Andrew John is a lifelong professional painter and teacher. His love affair with the inland waterways, their history, and welfare has spanned half a century. With his faithful four-legged companion, family and friends, he has journeyed, over the years, along nearly all the canals and navigable rivers of England. His many interests are diverse but painting, teaching, and writing are central to his life. He believes that as a pastime, painting en plein air with friends has few rivals. He has appeared in TV art programmes, been a popular contributor to art magazines and lecturer to art societies. He has published hours of art tutorials and has conducted an extensive programme of painting holidays throughout Europe.

Other works by Andrew John:

A Watercolour Journey (Hardback book) (ISBN 978 0-9561711-1-5)

A Watercolour Weekend (Tutorial CD)

Watercolour in Andalucia (Tutorial CD)

To our dear and faithful friend Douglas.

Andrew John

DOUGLAS' DIARY

AUSTIN MACAULEY PUBLISHERS™

LONDON • CAMBRIDGE • NEW YORK • SHARJAH

A CIP catalogue record for this title is available from the British Library.

ISBN 9781035852550 (Paperback)
ISBN 9781035852567 (ePub e-book)

www.austinmacauley.com

First Published 2024
Austin Macauley Publishers Ltd®
1 Canada Square
Canary Wharf
London
E14 5AA

I must express my profound appreciation for the assistance rendered in navigating the winding ways of our trusty narrowboat Albert, to all our visiting crew members. Also for the most helpful compendium of maps (Canal Companion series) by J M Pearson & Son for their guidance and information. With all this help we triumphantly conquered the staggering number of 300 locks, skilfully maneuvered approximately 100 swing bridges, and fearlessly ventured through eight mesmerising tunnels. We also braved the currents of six rivers, landed on only one sandbank and gracefully crossed seven majestic aqueducts as we ventured on this occasion, almost 500 miles through a fascinating history. My sincere thanks go to The Canal and River Trust, noble custodians of our treasured waterways, for their essential restoration and maintenance projects. Finally, my love and thanks go to my dear wife, Jan, our family, and friends for their patience in this production. In particular, Joan Fallon, Alan Johnson, Rachel Ward and Noah Price for their edits, guidance, encouragement and advice.

Table of Contents

Introduction   13

The Cast   15

Albert   17

Foreword   19

Chapter One: The Journey   21

Something's Up   23

We're Off   25

A Colossal Vessel   27

All at Sea   30

Auntie Rachel's House   32

Chapter Two: Lichfield Harecastle   35

Off to My Long-Kennel   37

Kings Bromley to Wolseley   39

Wolseley to Aston-By-Stone   41

Aston-By-Stone to Ham Heath   46

Ham Heath to Harecastle Tunnel   48

Harecastle Tunnel to Weedon Lock   51

Chapter Three: Wheelock Liverpool   **57**

Wheelock to Marston   *59*

Marston to Runcorn   *61*

Runcorn to Lymm   *63*

Lymm to Leigh   *66*

Leigh to Parbold   *69*

Parbold to Haskayne   *73*

Haskayne to Litherland   *76*

Litherland to Liverpool   *79*

Chapter Four: Liverpool Accrington   **83**

Litherland to Parbold   *85*

Parbold to Wigan   *87*

Wigan to Wheelton   *89*

Wheelton to Hyndburn Village   *91*

Going Nowhere   *93*

Skipton and Grassington By Car   *96*

Chapter Five: Accrington Leeds   **99**

On Our Way Again   *101*

Burnley to East Marton   *104*

Skipton   *106*

Skipton to Shipley   *109*

Shipley to Rodley   *112*

Leeds at Last!   *114*

Leeds, and It's Raining   *116*

Last Morning in Leeds   118

Chapter Six: Leeds Lincoln   **121**

To Stanley Ferry   123

Stanley Ferry to Ferrybridge   126

Ferrybridge to Junction Canal   130

Junction Canal to Keadby   133

Onto The River Trent   136

Lincoln City   140

Chapter Seven: Lincoln Lichfield   **143**

On The Trent to Newark   145

Newark   147

Newark to Hazelford Island   149

Rabbit Island   151

Ferry Boat to Nottingham   155

Beeston to Shardlow   158

Off to Burton   161

Almost Home   164

Kings Bromley   167

Afterword   **170**

Introduction

Allow me to introduce myself, I am a dog, my name is Douglas. I am an esteemed member of my family. I am no ordinary dog. In fact, I take great pride in my remarkable appearance. Picture, if you will, my long and silky ears, complemented by deep brown eyes that speak volumes. My jet-black nose, forever moist, adds a touch of elegance, while my glossy coat, a delightful blend of brown, black, and white, possesses a certain charm. I must say, I am a fine specimen of the tricolour variety. To complete this fetching picture, I have four white paws, a snowy white chest, and a tail with a white tip that wags incessantly.

From the moment of my birth, it became abundantly clear that I possessed an unparalleled handsomeness among my three brothers and three sisters. This bestowed upon me the privilege of being chosen by my beloved caretakers, whom I fondly and henceforth refer to as 'my Pets,' though they are, in truth, grown-up humans. The fortuity of our union extends both ways, for I recognise the good fortune we all share in my being selected as their loyal companion. Together, we reside in a charming and weathered house, nestled in a small village in the hills of Andalucia in southern Spain. From this vantage point, we are blessed with vistas that stretch far and wide, overlooking the majesty of the Mediterranean Sea in all its splendour.

Now, let me divulge a little about our escapades in England across the land and sea. We possess a long, thin barge known as a narrowboat, which serves as our annual haven during the summer months, when Spain enjoys scorching heat, while gentle showers embrace the English countryside.

In their advancing years, my Pets have assumed the roles of familial leaders, and it is within the pages of this diary that I have been directed to be the chronicler of our journeys and adventures on our narrowboat. I am a paw typist, but diligent and I have been assigned and have willingly undertaken the solemn duty of preserving our shared experiences, thus ensuring that my dear humans can relive the warmth of cherished memories. In case they forget.

Douglas.

The Cast

Douglas (that's me). A splendid blend of noble heritage, hailing from the proud and whimsical realm of goat herders, born unto the sun-kissed lands of Spain, albeit with an unconventional pedigree. My father was such a gallant figure, an esteemed long-haired Andalucian Shepherd, and my dear mother was a canine of great distinction and proudly represented the illustrious Welsh Border Collie tribe. Thus I am gifted with extraordinary good looks, unmatched intelligence and great herding prowess. When queried, I am known to jest and to claim a Golden Retriever lineage, or depending on my mood, an affiliation with the very rare Iberian Truffle Hound.

My Pets graciously assume the roles of my grown-up human owners—I prefer to think of them and usually refer to them as my Pets, they also consider themselves to be my carers or my keepers. The male figure, affectionately referred to by me as The Bearded One, stands distinguished. He is also known to other humans as Andrew, while his wife, the attractive female counterpart, is known as The Long-Haired One. This serves to establish the gender distinction and she is also known as Jan. Oh, how they adore me! In their artistic endeavours and leisure moments, they find solace, in painting pictures, particularly on holiday, while I, contentedly, indulge in the simple pleasures of walking, eating, sleeping, exploring, engaging in games of chase and catch the ball, find the ball, football and mouth-ball. Truly, these are some of my favourite things.

My short-kennel is a marvel that roams the asphalt highways. Yes, often also referred to as 'she,' similar to her larger counterpart, she is, in fact, an automobile. Yeti, as she is affectionately known. She grants me respite during our expeditions, offering a cosy space in which I may slumber, particularly on our journeys from one destination to another. Mostly in harmony, my Pets alternate the task of piloting this marvel, propelling us swiftly and often on extensive expeditions over many miles.

Albert

My long-kennel, residing in the heart of England, manifests as a narrowboat, stretching an impressive 58 feet in length. (about 18 metres). There is a clue in this title as she is only 7 feet in width (about 2 metres). It is upon this narrowboat, my holiday home, that I reside and help to navigate during our cherished holidays. Together, we embark upon leisurely voyages, traversing the ancient waterways that meander through the enchanting landscapes of England and Wales, along serene canals and winding rivers. Her name is Albert! Ah, the occasional quandary of gender confusion that arises when one endeavours to bestow a name upon a barge-type vessel.

Albert, not only shelters me and my cherished family but also extends a warm welcome to our dear friends who come to visit. She has comfortable guest accommodation offering all the comforts of home. I have my own cosy cabin with underfloor heating adjacent to my Pets' bedroom. Over the course of my existence, we have covered vast distances, exploring these treasured and historic waters.

Me

Foreword

In these diary notes, I will share with you a tapestry of tales about a particular voyage in Albert, my narrowboat, which I refer to as my long-kennel. I hope they will inspire your imagination. This voyage is known as The Outer Pennine Ring, a circular route stretching approximately 450 miles along eight canals and six rivers around England. This is my diary recording our adventures over the course of about 45 days, in August and September one year not so long ago. We travelled at a walking pace, which happens to be just one of my favourite things!

Chapter One:
The Journey

Something's Up

The air was filled with an unusual sense of anticipation as I found myself being whisked away to the dreaded vet's office. Oh, how vividly I recall my first encounter with that place, but I shall save that tale for another day, for it brings forth a well spring of emotions, rendering my eyes moist, or perhaps causing them to water slightly. This time, however, fate had a different plan for me. The kind vet lady, known to my Pets as 'Gemma,' greeted me with gentleness and compassion. Though I must confess, there was a momentary sting as she administered a needle to my neck. But, the pain was fleeting, I scarcely felt a thing. She then proceeded to listen to my heart, inspected my teeth and glanced at my bottom. *Maybe her style but rather undignified,* I thought. She seemed pleased with her efforts and to my delight, she rewarded my cooperation with a delectable treat—a beef-flavoured biscuit, broken up into little pieces which she administered gently, one by one. A result, I think.

Upon returning home, a strange atmosphere hung in the air. Something was afoot. My owners, or as I prefer to call them, my Pets, were engaged in a flurry of activity. They seemed to be packing away my cherished toys and toiletries into those portable boxes and bags that only emerged on rare occasions. A sense of unease crept over me. Could it be that they were preparing to send me away? Was I being banished from my beloved home? Did my visit to the vet have anything to do with this? I mustered my most sorrowful expression, hoping to tug at their heartstrings for some indication. Sadly, they were too preoccupied to notice my plea. Oh, the mysteries of human behaviour! What grand adventures await me in the midst of this upheaval? Only time or maybe the morning will reveal the true purpose of their actions. Until then, I shall remain ever watchful, ever curious, as I navigate this enigmatic journey called life and fall asleep.

We're Off

The next morning as always, here in Spain, the sun was shining but something was happening. I could feel it. On my customary walk with my bearded one, he did seem a little distracted and perhaps in a bit of a hurry. We greeted our friendly goats, and my friend Henrietta as normal. She is a donkey and lives nearby, and she neighed her *Buenas Dias* as we passed her shed. Nothing unusual here, but when we came back to our house, I found our home in a state of total disarray. All my beloved toys had now vanished, and even the boxes that cluttered the hallway last night had mysteriously disappeared. Alas, not even my cosy bed remained! I resigned myself to my usual tactic of looking utterly pitiful, half-expecting the dreaded words, 'No, you're not coming.'

But to my surprise and great relief, my long-haired one fitted me into my new going-away outfit, the one I received for my birthday. It is an orange device they call a harness that, I think, looks rather like a bra. Before I knew it, I was being packed into my trusty short-kennel, that propels us swiftly along the roads. And there it was, on the back seat, my cosy bed, awaiting my arrival. Happiness fills my heart. I am now excited, I recognise the routine, my memory is returning, oh how familiar it all is!

We are off again! Two hours of slumber, only to wake up in an unfamiliar place. After a brief interlude of football (in my case mouth-ball), they have a coffee and I get a drink of water, followed by two more hours of blissful sleep. Another awakening, another round of mouth-ball, and the exchange of seats between my Pets. Two hours more of sleep, then awakening to partake in yet another round of mouth-ball, more coffee for them. And suddenly, we find ourselves in an entirely new place, a big house where we all sleep together in a new room. I am reminded that we are at a place called a hotel—if you have never been to one, they are like very big houses with lots of bedrooms. This one has a large and very wide staircase, it bears the name Hotel Montermosa and nestles near the charming town of Aranda de Duero. Oh, it is delightful. They have a huge garden to play in, and I revel in the joy of it all. I am allowed to sit with my Pets under their table at supper time—I am very happy and excited.

Thus, I pen these words to you, from the comfort of my temporary abode. The adventures have begun, and I eagerly await what tomorrow shall bring.

A Colossal Vessel

Our routine is much like that of the previous day, I start with breakfast on a small terrace all together with my Pets. Actually, they had breakfast, and I walked my bearded one around the grounds for his early morning perambulation. It is good for him at his age. We are soon ready to continue our journey and once again, we gather ourselves inside my short-kennel. They assume their positions in the front seats, I surrender myself to slumber in the back and they take charge of driving. Today, the seat exchange occurred only once, and my opportunity for a swift game of mouth-ball was limited to a few brief moments.

I had just dropped off back to sleep when, all at once, we found ourselves in the midst of a remarkably old and picturesque village named Santillana del Mar.

I traversed the streets, attached to the lead that tethers me to either one of my Pets, this to keep them safe. I admire the many buildings that I can only explore through the wondrous sense of smell. I was not allowed entry, but the experience was nonetheless delightful.

Eventually, we made our way to a magnificent beach, with a great expanse of sand which signalled our arrival on the splendid northern coast of Spain. Ah, the exhilaration when I was released from the confines of my lead, instantly indulging in the delight of running around in a figure of eight (it is what I do on these occasions) and then rolling upon the damp sand. It was a truly glorious experience, one that left me only slightly moist compared to my bearded one. Oh, how fortunate I am to be spared the burden of trousers, for the sea pursued my bearded one relentlessly, chasing him up the shore. Alas, his agility, unlike mine, proved lacking on this occasion, which resulted in a manifestation of the long-haired one's displeasure. As for me, I simply shook off the excess moisture, while observing the bearded one's plight. I had to smile but with my countenance, this is barely discernible. It seems he had to navigate the land for the next few hours without the comfort of his socks, while his wet trousers stuck to his legs in a sorry state. A comical sight, indeed.

After our beach adventure, and lunch for them (I got nothing), we returned to my short-kennel and we set course for a place called Santander Port. It was there that I encountered a colossal, floating kennel, a sight I recalled from my past adventures. We had some time to wait, and of course, they wanted the exercise and so I played football (or in my case mouth-ball), with them, it pleases my Pets no end and, pleasing them, is one of my favourite things. After I had exhausted them with my superior ball control, we went back into my short-kennel and drove onto this colossal kennel vessel. This, by the way, is called a ferry. If you have never seen one, it is huge. Here is a sketch of it! There are lots of short-kennels joining us and we are all driving actually into this colossal ferry kennel, one by one we all gather together inside where there is an enormous car park or garage—at its bottom.

Here I found myself amidst a gathering of fellow canines and we had a special place but more about that tomorrow. First, we had to enter a strange, very small room, like a big upright box, the door opens and closes automatically and then opens again after a few moments, automatically, and we are in a completely different place! I think this is human magic. This is clearly a magic cupboard. I heard them call it a lift. I had to wear a nose bag when inside, they call this a muzzle. These are not nice things, they severely limit my sniffing. A very important facility for us canines, We are so much better at it than humans, thousands of times better. I have from past experience developed a cunning method of nosebag removal while my Pets are not looking.

Soon, we were all tired and ready for bed. We retired to a special cosy room, with beds, they called these bunks and these rooms are called cabins by the way, and I nestled between my Pets on my red bed. As I drift into sleep, embraced by the warmth of their presence, I eagerly await the adventures and look forward to tomorrow.

All at Sea

Dear diary, today unfolded with its own peculiar charm, we are surrounded by sea. As the morning sun greeted us, my bearded one guided me to a designated area called deck number nine! A special space was arranged for me and my four-legged companions which I briefly mentioned yesterday. We get there by the magic cupboard method. Interestingly, this area is called an exercise deck. Not a lot of room for exercise the way I like to do it! And, by the way, I am meant to be wearing that nose bag thingy called a muzzle but we have, most unfortunately, forgotten that. The absence of trees in this exercise area posed a challenge for many of my friends, but not for me! I am seasoned in the routine. I encountered no such difficulties. My bearded one, who is also used to this procedure kindly held up a broom, upright, with handle down brush up for me and some of my boymates, a clever aid to resemble a rather odd-looking tree, but it stimulated us in our endeavours.

Peering out into the vast expanse, all I could see was water, leaving me completely unaware of our location. I overheard my bearded one mentioning the presence of frogs, gesturing towards an invisible horizon. Alas, my eyes failed to catch a glimpse of them. Amongst the gathering of my kind, there were all sizes and shapes. I encountered a huge member of the Newfoundland Tribe. She was almost as large as my friend the donkey! I must confess, her imposing size gave me a bit of a fright. Although she wished to engage in play, I politely declined. Her paws dwarfed my own head!

At the end of our second day aboard, and as the daylight waned, our pleasant sea crossing was coming to an end. We are arriving at a place called Portsmouth. I found myself returned, via the magic cupboard method to my bed within my short-kennel at the bottom of this colossal kennel ferry vessel, in a sort of garage. Soon, I was much relieved when my dear Pets joined me. They sat in the front seats, and we set off once again, bidding farewell to the colossal kennel ferry vessel.

Strangely enough, we now found ourselves on the opposite side of the road. I suppose humans possess some knowledge of these matters.

As time passed, the air carried scents that stirred excitement within me. Instinctively, I knew where we were headed. And yes, we arrived at Auntie Rachel's house, a place I hold dear in my heart.

There, I am always greeted by two delightful small humans who relish every moment of playtime with me. Unfortunately, upon our arrival, they were already tucked away in their beds. In due course, we retired to our own slumber as well. Our bedroom, situated at the top of the house, holds a thrilling adventure for me. A spiral staircase awaits, and I, being ever so brave, have mastered its twists and turns and openness, a bit scary at first. The reward is the freedom to sleep wherever I please in a huge room they call an attic, and a luxurious hairy rug adds to the comfort.

Auntie Rachel's House

My dear diary, the events today started in a strange manner. The sun shone brightly overhead, casting its warm rays upon the land. However, to my surprise, my owners, the bearded one and the long-haired one, embarked on a sudden journey without me! They hastily climbed into my short-kennel, barely uttering a goodbye. I wondered how long their absence would be, as they had mentioned something about visiting their own vet for reasons unknown to me. Left in the care of Auntie Rachel (the daughter of my Pets) and my two small human playmates, Tillie and Poppy (the daughters of my Pets' daughter), we set off on a delightful adventure.

My day started with long explorations through the enchanting grounds of Sissinghurst Castle. The gentle breeze whispered secrets to us as we roamed, immersing ourselves in the beauty of nature. Upon returning to Auntie Rachel's house, Tillie and Poppy displayed such kindness towards me, showering me with an abundance of gentle grooming. Their delicate touch far surpassed that of my own Pets, I must say.

As the day drew to a close, my own Pets returned, seemingly in better condition after their visit to their vet. I was not told what was going on, neither did I want to know. We gathered around to enjoy a substantial supper, well they did, mine consisted of the usual fare of biscuits and half a tin of Chappie while they indulged in various beverages that seemed to fuel their lively conversations.

With contented hearts and stomachs, we ascended the spiral stairs once more, to sleep, perchance to dream, ahh yes that is exactly what I intend to do. I am excited.

Chapter Two:
Lichfield Harecastle

Off to My Long-Kennel

Today, with great anticipation, we rose early to re-commence our journey. It has been almost a week since we bade farewell to our humble home in Spain, and now a new adventure beckons in my beloved long-kennel. As we say goodbye to our dear family in Kent, the flurry of packing ensues, and I find myself comfortably settled on the back seat of my cherished short-kennel. Through their animated conversations, it becomes clear that we are going directly to my beloved long-kennel, Albert! She is, at her home mooring—a marina called Kings Bromley, near Lichfield in Staffordshire. This is about a three-hour journey by my short-kennel so it is time for a nice nap. A marina, by the way, is where a lot of long-kennels like mine stay. Ours is a very lovely marina, there are two very big lakes in a huge park with trees and grass and pathways. It is a playground of scents. I have quite a few friends who live there. It is very nice. There are squirrels and ducks and geese and swans and last year I nearly caught a rabbit. They are essentially, bouncy cats!

Oh, I am so excited at the thought of staying in Albert once again. It is from there that I can revel in the pursuit of ducks, the exhilaration of chasing squirrels, and the unparalleled delight of savouring the very finest goose droppings. These are the moments that bring me immeasurable pleasure, some of my favourite things, and I eagerly anticipate the long walks that await me in the days to come. The sights, sounds, and scents of our journey are positioned as I will soon be, on the stern deck (at the helm) alongside my bearded one assisting him to navigate, these are my thoughts as I fall asleep on the back seat of my short-kennel.

We arrive at Kings Bromley and we eagerly climb aboard Albert my long-kennel. She has her own special mooring platform curiously called a key! (I have since learned this has nothing to do with locks and is spelt in a funny way—quay). Sitting on this quay, out of the way, I can watch the frenzied activity of loading and unloading cases and boxes of provisions and numerous bottles. I saw my personal items being transferred from short-kennel to long-kennel, so I felt a little more relaxed and at the same time excited. Then, my long-haired one's sister Maureen and husband David arrive. They are our first guests and have come to see us in their short-kennel and they are joining us, to stay for some days on the early part of this adventure. They will be our crew for a little while. They brought along a delightful lunch, of which sadly I did not taste even a scrap! A little disappointing. Just a minor detail, of course. My bearded one busied himself with his head down the engine room, tending to the inner workings of my long-kennel Albert, while my long-haired one was busy stowing provisions for our voyage.

To my dismay, a man arrived to collect a considerable sum of money from my bearded one for he said, "Blacking Albert's bottom." The mere notion sent shivers down my spine, and I swiftly sought refuge in my bed until the man departed.

Kings Bromley to Wolseley

We cast off gently and without fanfare drifted slowly from our mooring after they had enjoyed the tempting spread Maureen had prepared and presented. None for me. The sun was shining, casting a warm glow upon the water as we glided slowly on our way turning north west as we left our marina, along our beloved Trent and Mersey canal, in my beautiful long-kennel. I was very happy and so excited. I positioned myself at the stern, observing with great interest, the fauna and flora as it floated by. My pet, the bearded one, and his brother-in-law David took turns masterfully steering our long-kennel as it slid gracefully through the smooth waters. I, meanwhile, marvelled at the serene countryside and scrutinised the ducks and the moorhen as they drifted tantalisingly close and slowly past my nose, they often spoke to me in passing, but I didn't catch what they said. They stayed just out of my reach.

As we journeyed, for little more than an hour, we passed through a small village called Handsacre, and then very soon came upon a sight that left me utterly astonished. It was a small town like no other, known as Armitage Shanks, and it was a haven of toilets! That is pretty well all there was. Everywhere I looked, stacks upon stacks of human porcelain toilets greeted my curious gaze and there was nobody there! Here I am relaying what I heard my Pets discussing: Armitage and Shanks have become synonymous with toilet plumbing, their trademarks adorning public conveniences across the globe. The site itself has a history dating back to 1817 when it became renowned for its sanitary ware under the management of one Edward Johns. It's fascinating to note the American term, sometimes used by humans 'going to the John' originated from this place, right here!

Allegedly.

After just another hour of cruising, we decided it was getting to be about tea-time and there being no rush, we had happened upon a tranquil spot to  moor for the evening. It seems in the middle of nowhere, surrounded by lovely countryside. I took my long-haired one, her sister, and her husband for a lovely amble along the towpath, I call these scent trails before we settled down for a satisfying supper and a well-deserved rest. Although we have travelled only a few miles on this first day with no locks (nothing to do with quays) more about these later. It has been a day of discovery and adventure. Here is our overnight mooring in Wolseley, Staffordshire. It was actually a very pretty spot.

Wolseley to Aston-By-Stone

I awoke early as the sun was rising and I could see through my porthole new vistas. I was so excited I rose from my bed (above the engine) and went to wake up my bearded one and coincidentally my long-haired one, both sleeping next door. I did this with the customary tongue-in-the-ear trick to remind my bearded one that I was ready to take him for his walk. Our regular morning exercise.

Our journey resumed in the early morning after a hearty and satisfying breakfast. For them! I had some biscuits and water. So exciting! We departed, passing the pretty village of Wolseley. As we cruised through the picturesque countryside, I found solace in sitting peacefully on the back deck keeping my bearded one company as he stood at the helm. Together, we marvelled at the abundance of wildlife that graced our path. He claims to have spotted a kingfisher, though I must confess I missed it. I had no idea that kings live in rivers. However, I did unintentionally partake in a culinary mishap by consuming half a butterfly, later identified, in a brief post-mortem examination, as a deceased 'Comma.' Ah, the joys of accidental lepidopterology. Herons, ducks, and moorhen dotted our way, providing a lively country scene.

The presence of several locks along the way offered me the opportunity to accompany my long-haired one on the shore, who by her choice, assumes the role of the opening and closing of these waterway portals. My bearded one, in the role of captain, meanwhile directs operations from the helm and manoeuvres my long-kennel through the locking process.

For those of my readers who have not experienced locks, please let me briefly explain: they are an ingenious way of lifting or lowering boats (like my long-kennel) up and down hills on waterways such as the canals like this one and all the others about which you will read much in this diary. Canals of course differ from rivers in that they, as waterways, do not themselves flow up and down anywhere! Hence the locks, I will explain later how they work. For the moment, I have to say it is important that my Pets and I all behave responsibly around locks and as I have mentioned my long-haired one assumes the major role at these locking events and I supervise her from a safe position.

Now, I will get this out of the way, I must confess to a small misadventure. At the start, I made a minuscule error in judgment and, maybe I was a little over-excited, I leapt off our long-kennel when perhaps I shouldn't have, resulting in a rather wet experience. (This was not at a lock, of course, I am very careful at locks). But, consequently, I have been assigned the task of wearing my bra (my going-away outfit, birthday present—whatever), at least for the time being, during some of our cruising moments. Allegedly and as just proven, this attire will facilitate my retrieval from the canal, should another waterborne misadventure occur. I shall endeavour to exercise greater caution. From last year's recollection, I now remember the routine, it is as follows: I remain in place, either on the boat or on the shore, or indeed the quay until given the signal that it is safe to jump, on or off depending upon my starting position. This routine momentarily escaped my memory, leading to my unfortunate lapse in judgement.

Between you and me, if I can share a word, dear reader, it was not entirely my fault. The signal, or command, that it is safe to jump has been established now for several years since I was very young, and it is the simple word 'Okay!' I know, on this recent occasion, I heard my bearded one chatting to my long-haired one when I am sure he said it, as he often does. I jumped, it was instinctive. How was I to understand it was not a command to me? They were surely just talking. I will be more attentive in future as I hear them use that word a lot. It is rather confusing.

Here's a bit of technical information that my bearded one wants me to share with you as we begin our voyage, just in case you don't know. The way locks work is so simple and so effective, my long-kennel weighs nearly 15 tons and we will raise it and lower it many hundreds of feet as we travel uphill or down on our developing adventure!

A lock is a long chamber with water in it, big enough to hold a very long-kennel, even longer than mine. There are about 1600 of these locks on the nearly 3000 miles of canals that there are in England and Wales. There are locks that can hold two long-kennels side by side. These are called double locks and we will use these later on our journey. We will also come across some very big locks that can hold many long-kennels all at once. Very exciting! I call these 'very big locks.' For the time being, we will be using single locks. All Locks contain water and have big heavy doors at each end. By using clever mechanisms in a particular sequence (which I do not fully understand) they can be filled or emptied with my long-kennel in it! That is what my long-haired one is demonstrating here, this is how she does it, she is winding with what is called a windlass to facilitate the filling or emptying of a lock and this is how we go up or down. Magic! A water-elevator!

Here I am watching my long-haired one opening a lock gate with her bottom, this is the correct procedure. I am just

checking that she is doing it correctly. She is leaning backwards on a heavy beam, as she steps backwards, moving the beam, she opens a very heavy gate to which the beam is attached. She closes the gate in the same fashion. Bottom walking.

To start, we will be going up, steadily for the first 30 miles or so as we head north, using some of the few hundred locks we will encounter on our long circular journey. When we reach the Bridgewater Canal at Preston Brook in a few days' time we go down a little. But, before that…it is so exciting! We will have completed five locks today and that means we have probably raised my long-kennel about forty feet.

As this day drew to a close, the sky darkened ominously while we found ourselves just south of the village of Stone, passing by a new marina near a village called Aston aptly named Aston Marina. Out of curiosity and for potential shelter, as it looked likely that rain was on its way, we decided to enter.  Coincidently, they happened to sell Adnams, a delightful beverage for humans that apparently is much admired, especially by my bearded one. Meanwhile, it did rain, but when it stopped, I found myself tied to a tractor as they embarked on a shopping expedition.

Please note it was a stable immovable tractor they did assure me, they made sure I was comfortable and from this vantage point I enjoyed the abundant attention that I received. I do seem to attract attention from some humans. The kind folk at the marina enjoyed my company so much that they invited us to spend the night, providing a convenient and safe resting place for my long-kennel and our weary souls.

Aston-By-Stone to Ham Heath

Today, as we commenced our journey towards Stoke-on-Trent, we were presented with a fair share of locks, although they were mostly grouped closely together (often called a flight of locks), this meant I didn't have to walk so far. I like walking, one of my favourite things but I was feeling rather tired. For a break, they entrusted me with the task of guarding our long-kennel while they embarked on a visit to the Wedgewood factory and museum, located near Stoke-on-Trent. I have no idea what they went to see or why but I was not allowed in, something about bulls and China shops, but I did not quite understand the relevance. I have a strong suspicion that I will be bestowed with this responsibility once again this evening when we find ourselves at Ham Heath. I overheard conversations suggesting a visit to see a Mr Toby Carvery who lives there apparently, whoever he is.

Please excuse the technical details that I have shared of the past two days at the end of this entry, as my bearded one insists on me keeping a log of our voyage. I hope this does not detract from your interest in my diary. To prevent it from becoming monotonous, I have been advised to provide synopses now and again of our adventures rather than just creatively writing about our exciting daily happenings! I think the purpose of all my labours writing this diary is so that my Pets can remember where they have been, why they went there and what was there and what they did when they were there!

As I have recorded, yesterday evening, we moored at Aston-by-Stone, and then on the following night, we found ourselves at Ham Heath. Throughout our voyage, the countryside has been breathtaking. The scenic vistas have been accompanied by the delightful presence of various creatures, making each moment a captivating experience. Dodging the showers has added an element of excitement to our days, although it has also left me feeling quite exhausted. It seems as though I have walked a considerable distance, which, I must admit, is one of my favourite things.

The weather today brought us a mix of showers and sunny spells, creating a warm and pleasant atmosphere for our journey.

For now, in the past two days, we have covered a distance of 28 miles, encountering 15 locks as we ventured north from our starting point on Friday afternoon. Our overnight stays were at Aston-by-Stone on Saturday night and Ham Heath on Sunday night. The countryside along our route has been nothing short of magnificent, captivating us with its natural beauty.

Ham Heath to Harecastle Tunnel

Toby Carvery! Well, he must have been a fine fellow and a splendid companion indeed, I feel sure! They all returned last night, brimming with delight, while I, diligent in my care of the long-kennel, received no treats save for a half-eaten hamburger for my unwavering watchfulness.

Exhaustion claims me, for I have traversed great distances on my four relatively short legs. This morning, they decided that since we found ourselves in the vicinity, a visit to Trentham Gardens was in order. And so, I dutifully accompanied them. Alas, I was compelled to remain on the lead, a rather tiresome restriction. This expansive domain was once the seat of the esteemed Dukes of Sutherland, yet it has now been generously bestowed upon the nation. Vast acres of resplendent gardens unfurl around a grand lake. We meandered through much of this enchanting landscape, and I, seizing the opportunity, anointed a multitude of diverse flora, as one does.

Thus, it was well past midday before we resumed our journey. You will not believe this, at the bottom lock on our ascent to Stoke-on-Trent proper, there is a Bone Mill! At a place called Etruria. Wow! I was not allowed to stop and investigate. I believe it is a museum now but in bygone days it was something to do with the manufacture of fine China. Maybe long ago I suspect inside, if not now, there was once a huge stash of bones! We are of course in the heart of the potteries, hey ho onwards we go. Proceeding through the town of Stoke-on-Trent. The most intriguing place it proved to be. Amazing I would say and I traversed much of it, on foot of course, as we encountered five locks, all close together ascending a formidable fifty feet. The crumbling remnants of a once proud industrial heritage enveloped us, evoking a sense of nostalgia. The fascination of my Pets was captured by the archaeology and architecture of the now mostly forsaken potteries, as well as the peculiarly shaped bottle kilns.

As for myself, I found greater intrigue in the fishermen we passed along the towpath, or to be more precise, their bountiful lunch boxes and delicious maggots, I lapped up a tongue full or two, much to the fishermen's displeasure, Well, they were presented in little open cartons on the ground. *Quite handy, thoughtful even and very tasty,* I thought.

As the evening gradually descended, we arrived at the south entrance to Harecastle Tunnel for our night's repose and preparation for the following day. Just a small piece of historical information:

This marks the second tunnel constructed at this very site, the first being crafted by the esteemed James Brindley in 1770. That's over 250 human years ago. Alas, it has succumbed to decay, brought about by subsidence. The tunnel we shall venture into tomorrow was fashioned by the famed engineer, Thomas Telford, and its completion in 1827—requiring a painstaking three years—stands as a testament to his craftsmanship. In the morning's early hours, we shall embark on a subterranean passage spanning one and three-quarter miles. In pitch black for about 45 minutes! I might not sleep well tonight, this tunnel is about 1,400 doggy years old!

Harecastle Tunnel
to Weedon Lock

Oh, the adventures I had today! Let me begin by recounting a rather significant mistake that could have had serious consequences if not for the presence of my going-away outfit. Prior to entering the tunnel, my bearded one took precautions to secure me (in case I was stupid enough to jump off in the dark, into the water and the black void—as if) by attaching my lead to a point on my long-kennel that was intended to allow me some freedom but contained within the confines of the small stern deck alone. Alas, his calculations for this restriction were off by about 18 inches! (Mathematics not being his strong suit).

It was at this moment that Peggy, a newfound and energetic friend from the Staffy tribe, called me out to play. Oblivious to my new safety device, in my excitement, she was very pretty, so I leapt off my long-kennel to join her. The next moment, I found myself abruptly, and most embarrassingly, suspended with my undercarriage just dipping under the water, rather like a fender on the side of a boat! My bearded one hastily hoisted me back inside, and to save face, to the apparently amused and watching audience, I pretended it was all part of the normal pre-tunnel entry and safety procedure.

At 8:30, precisely as planned, we were inspected by the man in charge of the tunnel, he had a big clip board and a small ball-point pen. He wanted to make sure our lights worked, and that we did not have our fire alight. and he inspected the red garment I was wearing and noted that I was secure. He seemed satisfied, he ticked the boxes, his checklist was complete, we were given permission to proceed, We were in front and therefore it was our responsibility to lead the waiting convoy of long-kennels to disappear under Harecastle Hill for at least forty-five minutes. We were cleared to enter the great dark hole. I thought for a fleeting moment, I would not want to meet one of those rabbits!

We are entering through the south entrance (my safety device has been adjusted, thankfully). My Pets, in fact, the entire human crew are adorned in waterproof gear, as they are well aware of the damp conditions inside the tunnel. Off we went, there were eight other long-kennels, venturing into the abyss behind us. It was black. Really black. When the last boat behind us had entered, I looked back and could just see a small crescent of white light, which was, I surmised, our entrance getting smaller. It was totally black ahead. Suddenly, there was a strange and frightening bang, and this light disappeared.

It was the sound of a big door at the entrance slamming shut! Now it was really really black and really really spooky. Then, the low moan of extractor fans started! Well, that was it, I have to confess, I was frightened. I indicated this to my bearded one and I was released from my position at the helm and taken to sit on my long-haired one's lap in the safety of our sitting room below decks. She stroked me for about forty-five minutes, as we trundled on in complete darkness, save for our somewhat inadequate headlight, until we emerged on the other side, greeted by fresh air and a downpour of rain. I was greatly relieved. I should mention here for my friends who are non-boaters, that a headlight's main purpose manifests in tunnels, not to show one the way, which it barely does, but to show the light to any oncoming boat that you are also an oncoming boat! In this case, happily, we were in a one-way system, all going the same way. After our eight-boat convoy had emerged at the north end the operation was reversed for boaters travelling southwards and so on every two hours or so.

Emerging on the other side, I noticed what a peculiar colour the water was, yellow ochre. I was told this was due to minerals. I know the area was rich in iron oxide as my bearded one knows about these things being a painter and stuff. Of course, on this side of the hill, it was raining and the rain persisted as we journeyed. This is a sketch of

the north side, in this case, the exit, where we came out—I am very pleased to say! We continued, encountering a succession of locks—one after another—for it seemed miles on end. In fact, we faced 20 locks over the next 10 miles. With each passing lock, I grew progressively wetter, as no one had thought to provide me with a raincoat. However, the bonus was that I was able to stay alongside my waterproofed long-haired one for most of the way. Walking, you see, is one of my favourite things and I know I will get a good rub down later with a towel, I just love that.

In the early evening, we moored for the night at Weedon Lock, a village spot conveniently located near a delightful Italian restaurant. Though the rain had ceased, the Pets and their friends, Maureen and David ventured inside for a lovely meal, while I remained on guard duty in my long-kennel. Alas, I was not allowed to join them, I got absolutely nothing but a bit of semi-chewed pork crackling that my bearded one brought back, which I presumed he had tried but not managed to fully digest.

Today marked the fifth day of our voyage, and the weather was mostly characterised by rain, overcast skies, and cool temperatures. Our journey took us from the Harecastle Tunnel to Wheelock, adding a distance of 10 miles and 25 locks. To date, we have covered 45 miles and interestingly encountered 45 locks, and that one very long tunnel!

As I conclude today's entry, I'd like to draw your attention to the map, this indicates our clockwise route. Perhaps you might find it of interest. It shows our complete journey from start to finish on this year's adventure of about 45 days. If you look on the map just north of Stoke-on-Trent, there is a tiny gap on our coloured route, which will be Harecastle Tunnel. This is where we have just been.

We started at the bottom of the map near Lichfield, and I have marked our approximate position at intervals every few days on our adventure.

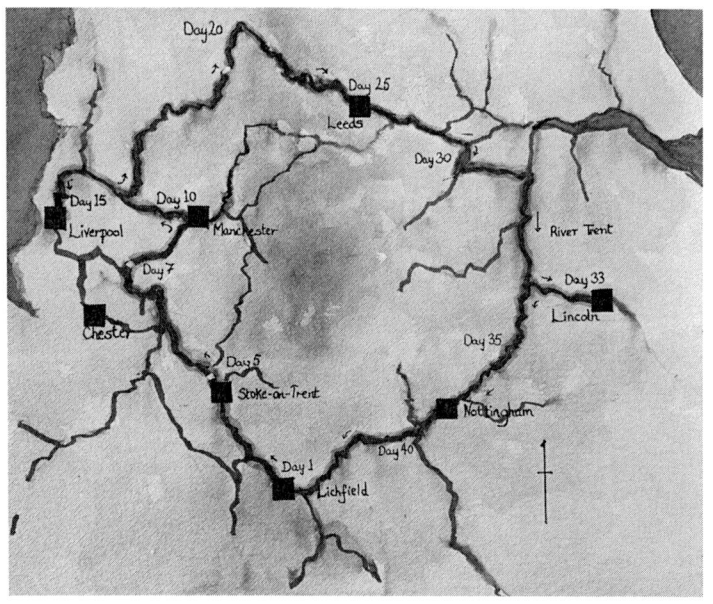

The Pennine Ring

Chapter Three:
Wheelock Liverpool

Wheelock to Marston

On the morning of day six, mist blanketed us from the surroundings as I took my bearded one for his early morning exercise. Despite the foggy start, there was a promise of a sunny day to shine through. While the rest of our party slumbered or attended to their morning rituals, my bearded one cast off, without any warning! I promptly assumed my command position on the stern deck by his side, ready for a tranquil cruise before breakfast. I love it at this time of day. Everything is so still and I watch, with fascination as the mist slowly rises to expose a new fresh vista.

We moored up for our morning meal (Chappie for me), and afterwards, we tackled nine locks in quick succession. This suited me just fine, as I had been well-rested and eager for more walking. The day developed beautifully, with blue skies and warm sunshine gracing our path. A bit of commotion ensued at Middlewich, where we encountered a series of three locks. A similar long-kennel to ours had broken down, and my Pets were kind enough to lend a helping hand in towing it out, a helping paw would have been more than useless, especially at this distance. I barked a few words of encouragement. Our good turn completed, we proceeded on through the bustling town of Middlewich and paused for lunch at a charming establishment called 'The Big Lock.' While my Pets enjoyed their lunchtime meal, I took up position in my usual spot under their table, content in their company and the odd scrap that perchance would fall to me.

Our journey continued through picturesque countryside, offering magnificent views over the vast Cheshire plain. As evening approached, we moored for the night in a peaceful wood just outside Marston. I led my Pets on a delightful evening stroll and even indulged them by playing fetch the ball (a variation of mouth-ball). Bringing the ball back to them always brings joy to their faces. I really like that, one of my favourite things.

We concluded the day by dining onboard, relishing the shared camaraderie. I like it when we stay on board. We watched some TV. It is not every night that my bearded one, who is in charge of this device, manages to get a signal. I don't watch much myself but apparently, a bad signal is usually because (he says), we are moored in a remote location sheltered by trees or other obstructions to stop the signal from reaching us, or it is because we are facing the wrong way, or it is due to the weather or, as in my super doggy opinion, it is because he has not managed to orientate our aerial correctly.

My synopsis for the day. At last, the sun has joined us. The day transformed to sunny and warm weather for a change providing the perfect backdrop for our journey from Wheelock to Marston and finally to Runcorn. As of this evening, we have covered a total of 70 miles, passed through 56 locks, and navigated through four tunnels. Quite impressive feat, if I do say so myself!

Marston to Runcorn

This morning, marking the seventh day of our voyage, we allowed ourselves a leisurely start, knowing we had ample time to reach our destination, Runcorn. This town boasts a mainline station connecting us to the well-known central hub of Crewe and thereby most other places where there are railway stations. Moreover, we were to conduct a change in the crew—David and Maureen would bid us farewell, returning to Lichfield back to our marina in Kings Bromley where they had left their short-kennel, while our friend

Rhylva, is set to arrive by train from her home in Eastbourne.

Our route for the day included three tunnels, but only a couple of locks and several elegant herons. Along the way, we passed the remarkable Anderton Lift. This is not like a magic cupboard. It is a massive steel structure, built over fifty human years ago, my Pets had experienced this on a previous voyage, prior to my arrival. It is capable of carrying two long-kennels plus the water they float in. One chamber goes up while the other goes down connecting the canal with the River Weaver fifty feet below. This, if one chooses, enables the users to delight in the wonders of the river, which connects with the Manchester Ship Canal and the Port of Liverpool and the Irish Sea. Not for us, we are taking the quiet long way round to Liverpool.

Continuing, we bade farewell to the Trent and Mersey canal at Preston Brook, negotiating our first descending lock to join the lock-free Bridgewater Canal. Our journey took a westerly turn onto the Runcorn branch, which initially sparked some trepidation, as the map guides were far from enthusiastic about this section. However, to our pleasant surprise, the journey proved to be most enjoyable and quite rural at times. The canal ultimately terminated conveniently near the railway station, positioning us for our upcoming crew change.

As the warm and sunny weather persisted, I treated my Pets to another long evening ramble before once again assuming my post on guard duty. They ventured out to meet a fellow by the name of Mr Two-for-one for supper. It seemed, as I heard them muttering, there was a shortage of pubs in the vicinity. I agreed to look after my long-kennel. I was quite tired, I wanted an early night and I wasn't invited anyway.

Runcorn to Lymm

First the summary: Day eight of our adventure: we were blessed with splendid weather as we voyaged from Runcorn to Lymm along the tranquil waters of the Bridgewater Canal. Today's leg of the journey presented us with a respite from locks, allowing us to navigate unimpeded. Our total tally now stands at 87 miles, encompassing 56 locks and four tunnels.

Last night I forgot to mention. Earlier in the afternoon, we encountered a dramatic incident in downtown Runcorn. This was when some poor soul was rescued from the water into which he had jumped, fully clothed and with apparent enthusiasm. It took a team of police men and women to retrieve him from the murky water semi-conscious and transport him by escorted ambulance to the hospital. It was disturbing to witness.

As evening approached, it was a welcome relief when a kind gentleman offered us sanctuary at The Bridgewater Boat Club, to stay overnight, free of charge. Nestled within the secure embrace of a gated mooring, we connected to mains electricity—a source of great delight for my long-haired one, as it facilitated her laundry endeavours. The pleasant weather allowed their garments to dry without hindrance. Meanwhile, my bearded one availed himself of the facilities, dutifully scrubbing the roof of my long-kennel, leaving it with a renewed air of elegance and him exhausted.

The change in crew transpired smoothly, Maureen and David were returned while Rhylva was collected, all thanks to the assistance of Virgin Rail from Runcorn railway station.

Soon after, we enjoyed a splendid lunch with Rhylva on board, we embarked on the next leg of our voyage, setting our sights on Manchester enroute to the end of our first stage destination, Liverpool where we would turn around to continue our journey north and eastwards across the Pennines.

Today's trip brought with it a welcome respite from locks, sparing me the opportunity to engage in my customary walks. However, I must confess that the morning proved enjoyable. While we lingered in Runcorn, awaiting the completion of their laundry duties, I took my bearded one for a wander around engaging in a playful game of find the ball (an exciting variation). Furthermore, I faithfully accompanied both of them on their urban sojourns as they procured provisions, walking the streets for a rather extended duration, which left me quite fatigued.

A late liquid lunch break beckoned in the mid-afternoon at a charming establishment known as London Bridge. I sought refuge under their table, a destination it might appear also pursued by my bearded one. His thirst appeared quite evident, which is understandable considering the exertion he endures standing at the stern of my long-kennel. It must be such hard work! 'Dragon's Fire' was the libation he imbibed, or so it was named. Fortunately, The Bridgewater Canal proved to be of a generous expanse, its generous width ensuring easy guidance from my bearded one on the stern deck. It proved to be a pleasantly serene, and picturesque cruise that led us safely to our overnight mooring at Lymm, where the ceremonial unveiling of a gift, a largish gin bottle took place!

Lymm is an extraordinary place, with an abundance of pubs—watering holes and restaurants, I call them all food houses. Solicitors seem to occupy most of the shops, while the pubs and restaurants themselves overflowed with patrons. They graciously allowed me to accompany them, and I found solace beneath their table as we indulged in the vibrant ambience of the surroundings at a noble (but rare it seems) dog-friendly establishment strangely named the Drunken Donkey.

Lymm to Leigh

First, a summary. The ninth day of our voyage commenced with splendid weather, though the sun intermittently hid behind clouds, gracing us with warm intervals. Our voyage from Lymm to Leigh added a respectable 23 miles to our grand total, which now stands at 110 miles and 56 locks and four tunnels.

Once again, I apologise for the mundane statistical report above, that my bearded one insists I include. Alas, it seems to be his peculiar obsession. Age-related, I suggest.

Lymm, as previously mentioned, proved to be a delightful little town, full of thriving pubs and restaurants. The section we explored appeared to be the old town, which exuded a certain charm, distinct from the less appealing, albeit not entirely uninteresting, suburbs as we ventured northeast, we were navigating our way into the vast expanse of Greater Manchester. Remaining on the expansive Bridgewater Canal, free from the hindrance of locks, we maintained a comfortable pace at the impressive speed of just more or less four mph. Along our course, we encountered a location with the appealing name of Waters Meeting and we crossed over and above the Manchester Ship Canal via a fascinating movable aqueduct—an intriguing and innovative piece of engineering.

It was like a big swing bridge full of water! You will recall The Anderson Lift could have given us access, via the River Weaver, to this industrial waterway now below us. This is really for large ocean-going ships.

Making a brief stop at a canal-side pub in Sale to partake in a refreshing mid-morning beer, our journey then continued through the enchanting village of Worsley—a delightful oasis amidst the urban sprawl. I disembarked for a leisurely stroll along the towpath with my long-haired one. Regrettably, this did not last for long, our surroundings were slowly becoming more dismal. My bearded one, at the helm of my long-kennel, was behind us, not in sight. He had yet to catch up with us. We slowed our walking pace allowing for his arrival at a bridge hole where we were safely collected back to the comfort (and I thought safety) of our long-kennel.

In our search for a mooring as a lunch stop, we ventured through a series of prospective stopping points that proved somewhat underwhelming, prompting us to continue onward. Lunch was instead enjoyed on the move—a pragmatic solution for our sustenance. Later in the afternoon, we came upon a rare tranquil countryside setting for our overnight mooring. Pennington National Park is just outside Leigh. Here, we will bid farewell to the Bridgewater Canal, transitioning to the Leeds Liverpool Canal, which will guide us on to Liverpool and subsequently, the next phase of our adventure, on to Leeds.

I led them out for a spirited game of football—a pastime that holds a special place in my heart because I am good at it. I use my mouth a lot, rather more than my feet. Although I am very nimble. We retired to the comfort of our long-kennel for supper, and a bit of TV, the signal was good in this urban proximity, and this was followed by bed.

Leigh to Parbold

Today marks the tenth day of our voyage, and it has been nothing short of eventful. My Pets have had to have their raincoats at the ready The weather was a mix of all sorts, keeping me on my paws, Our journey took us from Leigh to Parbold, covering eight locks and 12 miles. So far, we have travelled a total of 122 miles, passed through 64 locks, and navigated four tunnels. Quite the adventure.

I awoke my bearded one, the familiar tongue-in-the-ear routine and so the day began with a delightful early morning wander through a park near a magnificent lake. I had the pleasure of meeting two fellow members of the greyhound tribe, and together, we indulged in some lively play. Oh, how swift they were! They joined me in the fun game of chase-the-goose, this is a no-win game but fun.

Back on board and after a full-bodied breakfast for them, biscuits for me, we set sail, encountering our first obstacle— an imposing road bridge that required our attention. This caused quite a commotion, as my Pets struggled to operate the mechanism, much to the chagrin of the waiting road traffic attempting to cross over our canal route and pass on by. Despite the embarrassment, we eventually got things sorted, and the long convoy of road traffic we had created continued on its journey, some drivers waving at us, some in a strange way, as they passed on by and so did we. Soon, the rain made its presence known, just as we approached Wigan, not enhancing the sudden appearance of the first locks which, to our dismay, were secured to prevent vandalism.

My Pets, having entered the first lock found themselves unable to fill it or use the mechanism without a 'handcuff key.' With a tug on a long rope, they managed to dislodge our long-kennel from the lock we had hoped to ascend, taking shelter to reassess the situation while the rain poured down. They were soaked as they had failed to don their waterproof suits in time, but I, in my trusty fur coat, simply shook off the droplets.

After what seemed a long time to me, my bearded one consulted his trusty map ('always read the destructions first' my long-haired one often reminded him) and he discovered much to his surprise that a handcuff key was required for the next series of locks in Wigan. To deter vandals no less. Fortunately, after rummaging through his man drawer, he miraculously found the necessary key, which, he said he now remembers he had the good sense to purchase at the outset of our journey, it had just slipped his mind. This allowed us to proceed, albeit with a slight delay. We met no vandals. I kept looking for one, I don't think I saw one but then I don't really know what one looks like.

Our plan for the day involved meeting a friend of our friend Rhylva, who happened to reside nearby. The Crooke Hall Inn in Crooke was chosen as our rendezvous point, and to my delight, I was allowed inside to sit under their table. We were all quite damp from the rain, but the warmth of the pub and good company raised our spirits. I must admit, though, there were some unruly yapping dogs that tested my patience. I have to say under such circumstances, I tend to feel rather superior as I make no sound unless really stressed, I just observe. If you have nothing to say, say nothing—I say.

Following a satisfying lunch, for my Pets, and a dried biscuit for me, the sun emerged from behind the clouds, granting us the opportunity to dry off in the pub garden.

After bidding our friend Rhylva's friend farewell, we continued our journey through more substantial and challenging double locks. My long-haired one had by this time acquired help from another long-kennel who had joined us. They worked the locks together as I embarked on my own adventures, exploring the surroundings at a leisurely pace. The progress was rather slow, but it allowed me ample time to indulge in one of my favourite pastimes—chasing creatures or chasing anything. I had a brief encounter with some Canada Geese, but alas, they eluded me, and as a matter of record, they cheat anyway, if you get close to any one of them it will jump in the air and stay up there somehow, honking! However, as mentioned, their offering of poo is delicious. They are still feathered cats as far as I am concerned! One day, I shall catch one, mark my words.

As the day drew to a close, we moored for the night in Parbold. The rain had returned, prompting an early evening in. I really enjoy these evenings, lying in front of my wood-burning stove as it crackles away with the rain drumming on my roof, these are some of my favourite sounds. Then, after they had drunk their cocoa I got a biscuit, a human one, it was bedtime for me. I excused myself and climbed up the two steps to my room over the engine and after I turned around a few times (it's what I do), I dropped onto my cosy bed, ready for a well-deserved rest.

Parbold to Haskayne

Day 11 of our voyage. We have come a long way now from Staffordshire through Cheshire and now via Greater Manchester on towards our destination Liverpool in the Metropolitan county of Merseyside. The weather today was overcast, cool, and threatening rain. We have travelled about 130 miles, passed through 64 locks, and navigated four tunnels so far.

Yesterday's journey proved challenging, but we were fortunate to receive assistance and kindness from both locals and fellow travellers during our lock transits. Their help made a significant difference, especially considering the adverse weather conditions.

We began our journey at a relaxed pace, we had no pressing schedules, which as it happens was just as well. After a brief couple of miles, we encountered our first obstacle—a stubborn swing bridge that refused to swing.

It was a mechanical breakdown, causing some delays. However, after about half an hour of troubleshooting and resetting, the bridge finally cooperated. A few miles later, we faced another swing bridge that also refused to budge. This time, engineers were called to the scene, and we patiently waited. This delay gave me the freedom to explore, coming and going as I pleased. After an hour, the bridge was finally opened for canal traffic—that was us. Strangely, it seemed we were the only ones travelling along this stretch, which made me wonder if there was a message here hidden in the quiet waters. Next, we encountered yet another stubborn swing bridge. This time, it boldly stated that it was closed until 4:00 pm, and we arrived at 1:00 pm. The pub across the way provided some respite during our wait, although they were not serving food. Nevertheless, it offered a pleasant spot to pass the time, with plenty of liquid refreshments for my Pets.

Thankfully, the rain held off, and we still had no reason to rush and we finally made it through the third swing bridge at 4:00 pm, allowing me and my Pets time for a leisurely stroll before we were to continue our journey. This is where we had an amusing encounter. As I was walking my bearded and long-haired one a large brown mutt spotted me from the other side of the canal. My special look seemed to provoke him, and he began barking ferociously, creating quite a commotion.

His owner, clad in a string vest, which appeared rather too small for his large form, tried in vain to recall him as he raced along the towpath. I calmly strode along protecting my Pets ignoring him, which only seemed to irritate the mutt further. Completely out of control, he barked madly, and with such enthusiasm and with a mighty splash, he fell into the water. The sudden silence that followed was quite satisfying. I glanced back at his struggles to get out and left him to the extreme displeasure of his owner who appeared to express his frustration. He might have had a speech impediment or maybe he was in the business of trucking muck somewhere or something. Perhaps he was in the freight business.

Back on board, we completed our cruise, we had travelled about eleven miles throughout the day and we finally arrived at the Ship Pub, our rendezvous point with old friends Barbie and Mike. They came to visit us from their home, they lived not far away—in Southport. They will be joining us in a few days' time as our crew. I was surrounded by my friends in the pub garden, I had the pleasure of playing with Bob, he was from the Labrador tribe. As it was a dog-friendly pub, I was allowed to join them for dinner, although I must admit, I didn't actually get any food. Nevertheless, the company was delightful, and we enjoyed a pleasant evening together.

As I conclude my diary entry for today, I must say that despite the challenges and delays, our journey continues to be filled with fascinating encounters and memorable moments. I eagerly look forward to what the following days have in store for us. I have never been to Liverpool, although I think my Pets have.

Haskayne to Litherland

The weather is promising to be mostly sunny on our last leg to Liverpool. We are travelling today along the borders of Lancashire and Merseyside. We have travelled about 130 miles so far. What a great time! I took my bearded one for an early walk and then he cast off before breakfast as we still have about 20 miles to get into Liverpool proper. Every few miles now there is another swing bridge. I sat in my position on the stern deck watching my world go by. My long-haired one and Rhylva became quite experts at the operation of these bridges of which there seemed dozens. This involved a lot of walking for me and I generally was able to help them, by being observant, some of the operating systems were quite complicated and they were all different, some used keys, some were opened by mechanical means, some by the bottom walk routine as I described earlier. I don't think I contributed much but I kept them company. They like that.

All was going well until we arrived at Aintree, bridge number 9. There were no operating controls or instructions. A phone call to the Canal and River Trust revealed that this bridge, operated by staff only, did not operate on Tuesdays! O joy that is today! How strange…

In conversation with this authority (C&RT), my bearded one reported that despite our call to them yesterday, when we received their help and clearance, and after advising of our intention to enter the City of Liverpool, there had been no such warning of closure and we were rather disappointed. After some tactful negotiations and to cut this story short, we were rescued by lunchtime. Two very kind and friendly employees opened the bridge and sent us on our way with the promise that we would leave on Thursday and report to bridge number 6 at 09:00 hrs! We did not fully understand that but now sort of understand why we are the only traffic! We continued on our merry and solitary way.

It is apparent that canal traffic in and out of Liverpool City is, at this time, restricted, a state of which we were not but are now aware. Apparently, on certain days traffic is escorted in and on certain days traffic is escorted out. Nothing happens on Tuesdays!

A quick summary: My Pets seem to have developed a good relationship with the staff of the Canal and River Trust who assisted by opening several swing bridges specially for us. We were offered some secure moorings at their depot just outside the centre of Liverpool. We were advised it would be unsafe to moor in the centre of Liverpool overnight at this time, saying 'There have been issues.' We were told the moorhen swim in pairs and the fishermen use grappling hooks, for cars, bikes, trolleys, prams etc., no fish! Thus, we settled down thankfully for the night in secure moorings at the Canal and River Trust depot in Litherland.

My bearded one had clearly not done his homework. "Not entirely my fault," he mutters, in a grumpy tone of voice, as he goes on to explain that the information is published only on the Internet. Not easy access for him, he claims, being in a metal tube (My long-kennel) out of range most of the time (countryside) floating on water in a ditch (canal) under the trees (Bucolic) with not enough 'g' whatever that is! Oh, he can be so grumpy!

Litherland to Liverpool

Day 13 of our voyage brings us to Liverpool, and guess what? It's raining, quite seriously raining!

We navigated the canal carefully from Litherland to the centre of the city, specifically the Eldonian Basin. However, we were not permitted to proceed further on the Link to get to Albert Dock as we hadn't booked our passage. Also, we were advised not to stay at Eldonian Basin after dark. So we must return in daylight!

We left my beloved long-kennel, Albert, behind as it was still daylight and we walked to Albert Dock in the rain instead. It would have been a fascinating journey and somewhat drier had we been allowed to bring Albert—my long-kennel closer to the heart of the city.

There appeared to be ample space for mooring, but that's just how it goes sometimes. They made the effort. Here is a quick wet sketch of the Liver building in the rain.

We strolled around Albert Dock with its interesting array of cafes and restaurants, my Pets even visited The Tate Gallery, and we braved the rain to reach The Walker Gallery. My Pets were particularly interested in an exhibition being promoted there but it turned out that it had ended the previous Sunday! Luck doesn't seem to be on their side in Liverpool.

Upon arriving, soaked, at The Walker Gallery, it became evident that I, being a dog, would not be permitted inside anyway. This, I think my Pets anticipated, but, wet and weary, my bearded one asked the concierge at the door, as a special favour, if we could perhaps rest on the vacant bench just inside the entrance in the dry while my long-haired one with Rhylva explored the Gallery within. Dick Jobsworth (I believe that was his name), replied, rather abruptly I thought, 'Only blind dogs are allowed.' This seemed strange, for a visit to an Art Gallery. I have perfect vision and so anyway, our request was denied. My long-haired one and Rhylva entered the Gallery, and my bearded one and I waited in the teeming rain, just outside the entrance, peering in at the concierge, through the automatic doors. Strangely, the more we peered at him on the other side of these doors, or to be more precise, the more we waved at him, the more the doors opened and then closed again. I found that quite amusing, I think the concierge found it quite irritating. After a while, he said we could come in and sit on the seat inside in the dry.

Finding a place for lunch with a wet dog as a companion proved to be just as challenging, and I couldn't help but feel somewhat of a burden by this time. However, we stumbled upon 'The Cavern,' one of Liverpool's renowned venues. My bearded one, clearly mustering up all his charm, negotiated with the lady proprietor, and it was agreed that we could all, as a special favour, have lunch. I was on my best behaviour and under direction from my bearded one, displaying an expression of forlorn, I was duly tucked under their table. It was a lovely visit and most interesting, they kept mentioning beetles but I couldn't see or find any and so I had nothing to eat or play with as usual.

After lunch, as it was getting late, we hailed a taxi to take us back to my long-kennel via the station to drop off Rhylva. I was quite tired. We were anxious to get back before dark, as we had been advised. This proved rather difficult as the first taxi we challenged was not a dog-friendly taxi. I had not experienced one of these before. After he realised that I was at the party, he refused our admission! Now, I was beginning to feel very unloved. But my bearded one and my long-haired one reassured me that I was really much loved and I should not worry about some humans being very strange.

Anyway, happily the next taxi we ordered assured my Pets and our friend that he would be very happy to accommodate all of us including me. He duly whisked us off to the railway station, we said goodbye to Rhylva and we went on to our long-kennel waiting at our mooring at Eldonian. You will recall, we were advised against mooring here overnight so we took this advice and my bearded one fired my long-kennel engine and off we went back to our secure moorings as fast as we could (4 mph) to our secure moorings at Litherland Village, thanks to C&RT. Tomorrow we start on the next leg of our journey to Leeds.

Chapter Four:
Liverpool Accrington

Litherland to Parbold

We have a crew change today, we have been out over two weeks now and today we welcome our new crew members on board, our old friends Bob and Sheila, who are both experienced boaters and painters. They joined us this morning after some careful planning, at the Ship pub bridge. It is still raining. We have a 15-mile journey ahead with 12 locks and a few swing bridges and so there is a fair amount of muscle required. Bob is flexing his!

As we set off, we knew we would be delayed at that swing bridge again that only opens at 4:00 pm. Arriving around 2:00 pm, we took the opportunity to enjoy a delightful lunch with special pies that our friends Barbie and Mike had left with us from their visit. Unfortunately, I didn't get a taste of those special pies. Instead, I ended up doing a lot of extra walking in the rain, accompanying my long-haired one and our friend Sheila. They seemed to enjoy it, so I stayed by their side. Occasionally, I would run ahead to catch up with my long-kennel, which was at this time a bit faster than us. However, without the 'Okay' word, I couldn't jump back on board, so I would have to run back to them. It was quite tiring, back and forth, back and forth. The lock and bridge transits all went smoothly and it was a long but productive day.

For our overnight stay, we found a lovely wood near a bridge to moor. My bearded one and his friend Bob seem to think it would be a potential painting location if they manage to wake up early enough. They are too tired tonight and tomorrow promises to be a full and exciting day as we will be taking my long-kennel up 200 feet and navigating through 28 locks. It's expected to be a busy day of adventure. These water elevators are an amazing invention.

Parbold to Wigan

Parbold to Wigan. We left early and the weather was threatening rain and duly delivered it in sudden and quite violent bursts. We departed from our tranquil rustic mooring and made our wet way to Wigan, which was a journey of just a few miles. Along the way, we encountered some easy swing bridges and a few locks. In three of those locks, we were accompanied by another long-kennel, although there were not any of my kind on board, only humans.

Wigan, it seems, has been left behind by time, and I must say that we should consider leaving it behind too. You can see a sketch of Wigan Pier as it appears today to get an idea. But in any case, we have a hard day's work ahead and so we must not dilly dally, up 25 Locks we go!

Upon our arrival at the foot of the locks, the sun was shining, hooray! This marked a major crew change, albeit a temporary but rather necessary one to add some muscle for our ascent. At 1:45, my long-haired one and her friend Sheila left us, and in their place came Mike, our friend from Southport. This was a plot orchestrated by Mike's wife, Barbie, and my long-haired one. With Sheila, they went off to engage in some human lady therapy pursuit, shopping I think it is called. So, it was just us four blokes—me, Bob, Mike, and my bearded one—taking charge of this significant event which I supervised, while my bearded one, in his self-proclaimed captain status, piloted my long-kennel. This left Mike and Bob with the exciting and most enjoyable task of opening all 28 locks. It took them a good five hours to reach the top, and by the end, I was utterly exhausted as I was with them all the way. Throughout, I kept them company and I had to socialise with many of my kind too, exchanging smells and stuff.

When we reached the top, the sun was still shining, and to our delight, there was a pub! We took the opportunity to refresh ourselves. After he was restored, Mike bade us farewell and went home to his house in Southport for a well-earned rest leaving just me, Bob, and my bearded one. They enjoyed their supper while I had mine in my long-kennel, followed by a long sleep.

Wigan to Wheelton

A summary of yesterday, our 17th day, a lot of locks and a lot of help. After Mike had gone home my bearded one and his friend Bob were left to their own devices, they opted for a pub dinner.

As for me, I had my usual supper on board, a satisfying meal of half a tin of Chappie and a handful of biscuits. We all retired early, thoroughly exhausted from our strenuous ascent from Wigan.

This morning, we rose bright and early. After my bearded one and his friend Bob enjoyed a delicious breakfast that filled the air with delightful aromas, and I had my dry biscuits, we set off on our cruising adventure, enjoying the warm sunlight. Our mission for the day was to find a suitable pub for lunch, where we would arrange for my long-haired one and our friend Sheila to return and join us after their excursion, courtesy of Barbie and Mike. They were acting as our taxi service, as they live nearby.

After a couple of hours cruising, we had located two pubs on the map. Unfortunately, one of them didn't serve food, and the other didn't serve anything. It was boarded up, leaving us disappointed and hungry and wouldn't you know it, just as our search was in full swing, the rain started in earnest. We brought Sheila and my long-haired one back on board while we continued our search by canal and road for a much-needed pub, cafe, restaurant—any human food house!

We were not having much luck, so we called in at a marina to refuel, where we discovered a cafe that boasted a seven-day-a-week operation—with a notice displaying 'except Sundays!' How strange, would you believe it—today is Sunday and it was closed! It was here that we bade farewell to Barbie and Mike anyway, they left without a proper lunch to drive back to their home in Southport.

Undeterred by the rain, we continued our journey and, except me, all were dry and dressed in their waterproof suits.

An opportune dry spell led us to a flight of seven locks at Wheelton, a sight that filled me with joy. I relish the opportunity to stretch my legs, socialise, and experience the lively atmosphere of lock transits. I find them fascinating. To our delight, another long-kennel joined us for the ascent, making the experience all the more enjoyable and certainly easier for our crew. With swift progress, we reached the top of the flight in no time.

At long last, we stumbled upon a charming pub, which seemed to hold the promise of a satisfying meal. My owners and their friends were positively giddy with excitement about dining out, and I was given a treat to keep watch over the long-kennel. They returned after less than five minutes, rather disappointed to discover that the pub, named 'Top Lock,' ceased serving food at 7:00 pm. Despite this setback, The Pub offered a safe mooring and they managed to salvage the evening by engaging in a pint or two, a home-cooked meal and an exhilarating game of Rummikub. As for me, I found solace in a peaceful slumber.

Wheelton to Hyndburn Village

The day began with rather more than a heavy drizzle, and I had no desire to venture outside for my morning ablutions. The sound of raindrops drumming on the roof made me feel all the more snug inside. However, once the humans had completed their strange morning rituals, the rain had subsided, and I accompanied my bearded one on his walk.

Despite the wet start, the weather gradually improved, and the morning grew warmer and brighter. As we returned to my long-kennel, patches of blue sky peeked through the clouds, while the seductive scent of bacon wafted from the galley. Alas, my hopes for a breakfast treat were soon dashed, and I settled for biscuits—again. And so we meandered on our way to Blackburn, it was a delight to the senses with not a hint of industry to interrupt our vistas of hills, trees and fields. My long-haired one and her friend Sheila accompanied me on a lengthy ramble, immersing themselves in the picturesque surroundings.

Then, we arrived in the heart of Blackburn, where a flight of six locks awaited us. To our delight, we joined forces with another long-kennel, which boasted no less than four companions of my kind on board. Among them was a mammoth-sized hailing from the fox hound tribe, while the others whom I only heard, remained confined to their long-kennel, unable to participate in our playful escapades.

A stop for provisions was necessary, obliging us to go into town. An abundance of bottles made its way back to my long-kennel, while my bearded one diligently removed a plastic bag, half a raincoat, some fishing line and a bra that had entangled themselves around the propeller. Quite the peculiar assortment, I must say.

Our search for a human watering hole or eating house proved fruitless, and so we decided to moor up in the serene countryside near the village of Hyndburn. As my Pets and their friend Bob set about their artistic endeavours, wielding paint brushes and easels, I assumed my duty of patrolling the area, up and down, keeping a watchful eye. We encountered many of my kind, strolling with their owners along the tow paths, all enjoying these fascinating scent trails as much as I do. We had a nice restful evening on board enjoying each other's company.

Going Nowhere

Oh, what a day it has been! The adventures and mishaps continue on our voyage. Today, we found ourselves in Oswaldtwistle, an area with a name as peculiar as the events that unfolded. Let me tell you how this day started for my long-time friend, Bob, always an early bird. As the first rays of dawn stretched across the horizon, there stood Bob, diligently arranging his easel, eager to capture the essence of our journey with his watercolours. But fate had other plans in store. Out of nowhere, a strange noise was developing and getting louder about to shatter the tranquillity of Bob's peaceful morning. Lo and behold, a pack of wild horses came charging along the towpath, their hooves pounding the ground with untamed fury! Poor Bob's serene artistic endeavour was swiftly disrupted. With spontaneous and nimble reflexes, Bob found safety atop my long-kennel.

From that vantage point, he witnessed his unfortunate easel being swallowed by the calm waters of the canal, disappearing into the depths below. Ah, the adventures we encounter in life's meandering journey! Bob's misadventure with the runaway horses shall forever be etched in our memories, a colourful addition to the canvas of our floating escapade.

But the day's drama didn't end there, my friends. As we set off, from our mooring at Aspen Bridge our engine decided to join in on the excitement, displaying a most peculiar behaviour—a missing beat. Bob and my bearded one, our captain, our resident engine whisperer, suspected fuel starvation as the culprit. Recalling that only a few engine hours ago we had fuelled up at a suspicious location advertising seven days a week service except Sunday! The diesel pump situated adjacent from which we had loaded our fuel tank, was equally suspicious. The possibility that the purity of this recent intake could have been suspect did occur. A call was made to a mechanic named Steve, whose boatyard was located a couple of miles ahead on our journey and we made our way, limping to his workshop.

I should mention that this boat yard (where I could see no boats) was elevated some feet above the canal water and accessed by a slightly dodgy metal ladder arrangement. *Not a lot of good for me,* I thought, *but then I must not interfere.* We had an urgent situation as it turned out. Steve, at his workshop in Accrington, the saviour of engines, performed his diagnostics and agreed with our initial assessment. The fuel filters were duly changed, and the bottom of our fuel tank was syphoned, all while the engine proudly displayed its relatively modest 1290 hours of service. Quite the accomplished engine, I would suggest.

While Steve was tending to our mechanical woes, I seized the opportunity for a grand adventure. Accompanied by my long-haired one and Sheila, our dear friend, we embarked on a lengthy ramble to explore the picturesque surroundings. Little did we know that this stroll would turn into an extended stay.

Oh, the suspense! It turned out that our engine was not content with just a missing beat perhaps caused by some dirty fuel. Upon closer inspection with a tiny mobile TV camera, a surprising piece of high tech. diagnostic, it was discovered that three crucial bolts, holding our quite heavy 35 horsepower engine in position, were—'in perilous danger of imminently collapsing' announced Steve, sucking in his cheeks with the appropriate noise and at the same time, scratching his head and simultaneously his stomach. He continued sombrely, '—to rectify this mechanical malady, the engine needs to be lifted, and the old bolts are to be replaced with shiny new ones!' A bit of an issue and a daunting task that would result in an unscheduled three-day downtime, in his estimation, altering our carefully laid plans. "To risk an onward journey," he continued, in case we were in doubt "…would be extremely hazardous."

Rain has been our constant companion for some time now, as if the heavens themselves conspired in our misfortunes to deter us from our peregrinations. Yet, we find solace in the fact that a vigilant mechanic averted a potential disaster in the nick of time. Tomorrow, promises more revelations and twists in our odyssey.

Just as a matter of interest, dear reader. If you refer back to the map, we are almost exactly at the top of our route, our most northerly point close to the tiny village of Accrington. We are now about halfway on our journey and about as far as we could possibly be away from our home base back south where we started.

Skipton and Grassington by Car

Fear not, for we have procured a vehicle, a short-kennel no less, to continue our explorations while my long-kennel languishes in the boatyard. Today, we ventured forth to the town of Skipton. Although our hope was to visit Skipton aboard my long-kennel, as indeed we will, but for now, fate had other plans. We cruised the streets in our borrowed short-kennel, embarking on lengthy walks through the town's charming alleys. We sought solace from the rain in a pub garden its welcome shelter providing respite as we dined beneath an almost protective tarpaulin, warmed by heaters. Skipton, with its bustling markets and picturesque architecture, captivated our hearts. But the adventure did not end there.

We journeyed to the enchanting village of Grassington, an area we would almost certainly have missed by staying on board my beloved long-kennel, it proved to be a place of ethereal beauty. We marvelled at the famed waterfalls, their cascading torrents mesmerising our senses. And, oh joy, for during this part of our day, the rain graciously ceased its relentless downpour.

Steve.

Upon our return to the boatyard, we were greeted by the sight of Steve industriously working on my long-kennel. The engine, suspended by straps, stood as a testament to his efforts. The gearbox was separated and connecting pipes lay scattered—a scene of mechanical confusion. Steve, determined and steadfast, with his head down, crack displayed, wrestled with nuts and bolts,

occasionally embellishing his struggles with colourful language that seemed to tickle my Pets bemused ears. All the while my long-haired one was supplying him with copious cups of tea.

Nobody but me seemed to notice that this just happened to be my bedroom, all in suspension! As I may have mentioned before, I am very fond of my cosy bedroom and its comfy bed that sits above the engine of my long-kennel, keeping me cosy. I am grateful for this provision of underfloor heating, something I find immensely comforting. What now? I ask myself where am I going to sleep tonight? Does anybody care? O Joy, My long-haired one must have read my thoughts, for she had made my bed up on the foredeck right next to the lounge from where I could watch TV with my Pets if I so wished. I was very happy.

At the stroke of 8:00 o'clock in the evening, a triumphant announcement pierced the air—Steve had triumphed over the major challenges and expressed confidence in completing the repairs by tomorrow midday. What a pleasant surprise! My owners beamed with delight, their gratitude overflowing as they offered Steve another cup of tea. A small token of appreciation for his dedication and hard work. And so, we find ourselves in a momentary state of respite. Tomorrow promises renewed hope, a reconnection with my beloved long-kennel.

Chapter Five:
Accrington Leeds

On Our Way Again

Happy days have returned. As the morning dawned, raindrops persisted in their relentless rhythm upon my long-kennel. Reluctantly, I stirred from my deep slumber on the foredeck. Here I have a canvas roof with a zipped flap for easy exit, the better to accompany my bearded one on his walks. To my surprise, the rain had momentarily ceased, and I found delight in our amble in the fresh morning air. Upon our return, a sight of great significance greeted us—Steve, the skilled craftsman, laboured in the engine room, adding the final touches to restore my long-kennel to its former glory. Oh, the sweet sound of progress! Patches of blue adorned the sky, and a sense of anticipation filled the air. My hairy friend Bonnie, a Belgian Shepherd of great playfulness, joined our company, belonging to none other than Steve himself. Alas, a near tragedy unfolded before our eyes!

Bonnie, in her fervent quest to find me upon my long-kennel, for I was not in my normal place, met an unfortunate accident and tumbled into the canal from her vantage position some feet above us! The unmistakable thump echoed through the air as she bounced off my long-kennel and fell into the water. The alarm was raised, and with swift action, Steve and my bearded one rescued her from her watery predicament.

Though her pride suffered a blow, her physical well-being remained intact. I know I am very attractive but I wonder if there is any limit to which the females will go to get my attention? I hope I see her again.

By the stroke of 1:00 pm, my long-kennel stood in pristine condition—engine mounting bolts repaired and shining, all connections secure. Bedroom restored. My long-haired one busied herself with further washing while we were connected to mains electricity and all the while a sense of contentment settled upon us all. At precisely 2:00 pm, we bade farewell to the skilful Steve, a man somewhat enriched not only in monetary terms but also in the satisfaction of a job well done. With some excitement and much relief, we cast off and set our course for Burnley. I glanced back at Bonnie, I think we definitely have some connection, hey ho!.

Throughout the afternoon, the weather remained cool, dry, and overcast. Accompanied by my long-haired one and our friend Sheila, I explored the towpath with mainly my nose as one does, as we embarked on a leisurely stroll that seemed to stretch for hours yet, in their company, the time flew by, in truth, I enjoyed every minute, walking, as I am sure you know by now, is one of my favourite things.

Our path led us to a tunnel, named Gannow Tunnel where we stopped and waited to rejoin the safety of my long-kennel that was following us behind. I don't really like tunnels, they are not among my favourite things although this one was not very long. Emerging on the other side, we were met with a huge deluge of rain, and a transformation unfolded as we entered the bustling town of Burnley. We meandered through a tapestry of mills and weaving sheds, remnants of a prosperous era that whispered stories of bygone days. Suddenly, like a hidden oasis, we found ourselves in the midst of picturesque countryside, nestled beneath the shadow of Pendle Hill. At 1831 feet, it was a beautiful sight and it was there that we moored for the night, finding some welcome peace and quiet.

Burnley to East Marton

Today has been an absolute delight for me as I wandered for countless miles alongside my long-haired one. Our meandering journey through Burnley proved to be a delightful and surprisingly rustic experience. I took up the role of supervisor at numerous locks, and as we descended from the summit level, we found ourselves on a thrilling descent towards Leeds. Not only were we leaving the summit level of The Leeds and Liverpool Canal, but we were also leaving the County of Lancashire and arriving at the County of Yorkshire. There seems to be some disagreement among the locals as to the precise location of this border crossing. Nevertheless, the weather has vastly improved!

Having scaled the Pennines from Liverpool, the exhilaration of this voyage is immeasurable. The scenery in every direction is simply breathtaking, evoking a sense of being on top of the world. I estimate our distance from Leeds to be approximately 40 miles, which places us around 70 miles away from Liverpool. It feels like an eternity since we departed from there. We are now about halfway on our journey on our grand circular voyage.

We also ventured through a long, dark and sombre tunnel named Foulridge. The journey through this tunnel lasted nearly half an hour, and I must admit, it made me quite anxious. The darkness enveloped us, with water ominously dripping around us. Seeking comfort, I retreated inside my long-kennel until the ordeal was over. On the other hand, my bearded one and his friend Bob seemed to revel in the experience. They think that this is the moment we are moving from Lancashire to Yorkshire,

We find ourselves moored in the picturesque hamlet of East Marton, we are now definitely in Yorkshire, nestled along the travellers route known as the Pennine Way. This quaint village boasts a population of hardly more than 20 on a good day, or so it would seem. Our choice of stopping point was primarily driven by the presence of a delightful and dog-friendly establishment known as The Cross Keys. Not only do my Pets yearn for the comforts of a human watering hole this evening, but it is also essential to facilitate a crew change.

Summary, of about our 25th day: I can't accurately count past 20. We bade farewell to Bob and Sheila, yet joyously welcomed Mike and Barbie back again as our new crew and companions. This transition will take place tomorrow, and the environs of a fine pub provide a civilised backdrop for such proceedings. Tonight, therefore, marks our final supper with Bob and Sheila. I am invited to partake, destined to find my place beneath their table. Nonetheless, I have already enjoyed my Chappie meal and biscuits aboard my long-kennel, but any additional treat would be most welcome.

Skipton

I must declare that this morning I have seen the most torrential downpour of my entire existence! Rainfall of colossal proportions, accompanied by icy pellets that my long-haired one referred to as 'hailstones'—Alas, I find no joy in such weather! I really don't like water except to drink. This deluge transpired while we were navigating a series of locks just outside of Marton. I got very wet.

It was after we had said goodbye to Bob and Sheila and in their place just welcomed Mike and Barbie, in East Marton. With hopeful skies, albeit somewhat damp, we had set off towards Skipton. It was as we approached the first lock, paired with another long-kennel, it got quite dark and a thunderous rumble filled the air, instilling fear within my heart. Moments later, the heavens unleashed this relentless downpour, drenching everything in its path. My devoted long-haired one attempted to shield me by pushing me under a bush as we were sheltering in the trees, but alas, both she and I were soaked by the deluge, as was everyone else, there was much scrambling aboard. Lightning flashed and thunder clapped, this is quite disturbing when sitting huddled inside a 58 ft metal tube on water. We were spared, as indeed were all the other long-kennels whose occupants had taken the same steps, to stay inside while the storm raged. I certainly do not like hailstones.

Despite this drama, the heavy rainfall persisted with a lesser intensity, as indeed did our journey. After approximately two hours, the rain subsided to almost nothing at all as we reached Gargrave, where we sought respite and sustenance. Hot soup proved to be a welcome solace accompanied by a change of attire for my Pets, I received a rubdown, which I really, really enjoyed—one of my favourite things, We transformed this into a long leisurely lunch break, and when we felt ready and dry once again, we continued towards Skipton and the sun made a feeble attempt to emerge.

As the weather had improved, this was a rare opportunity. I took my long-haired one with her friend Barbie for their afternoon saunter. Here I must admit to a bit of playful mischief that took an unexpected turn. As fate would have it, we were passing a large field inhabited by a great number of rather (in my opinion) inactive bovine creatures, much bigger than me but their coats were the same as mine, mainly black and white. I felt it was my solemn duty to infuse some excitement into their rather mundane munching routine. In any case, they were all lying down and all they seemed to do was chew, munch, chew, and in my enthusiasm, I thought I should perhaps liven things up a bit. Just a simple wire was the only thing that separated me from these rather inactive but potential playmates. Well, I said to myself, "Here we go!"

As I leapt to clear this obstacle, it was in mid-flight that I was met with a massive and unexpected jolt in a rather sensitive region of my person, causing me on landing to involuntarily run around and bark a bit. Such was this unexpected commotion that it alerted my newfound companions and they proceeded to rise as one and to scatter in a chaotic display in all directions, leaving me stranded alone in their field, pondering the peculiar turn of events. Regrettably, my long-haired one failed to grasp the full extent of my misadventure. With an air of gravity, she demanded my immediate return from what she perceived as an exuberant rendezvous with the bovine folk. Thus, I was swiftly summoned back.

However, I had already determined that the stampede was not really my fault and anyway my inclination to liven up their existence had considerably waned. Crossing that wire again, clearly a black magic one, was out of the question. Instead, I endured the ignominy of being carried back by my bearded one, who had been assigned the task of rescuing me from the field and escorting me back to my long-kennel. Here I spent the remainder of the afternoon pondering the lack of appreciation from my Pets for my comedic efforts.

By 7:00, in the evening we arrived in Skipton, where, through great good fortune, we secured the very last mooring capable of accommodating the 58-foot expanse of my long-kennel. While my Pets indulged in a refreshing gin and tonic, I contented myself with a serving of Chappie and biscuits after which I gratefully went to bed for an early night, dreaming of fields of munching cows and left them to it.

Skipton to Shipley

 This is the weekend, when vast quantities of boating enthusiasts take to the waters, today, basking under the sun's warm embrace. The waterways are teeming with people and I too have spent much of my day exploring these long towpaths and scent trails. I've encountered numerous fellow canines doing the same as me sniffing, a fine collection and a diverse array of different tribes. It's been a pleasure to exchange smells and friendly chats, although I must confess that I don't comprehend all that is said—me being of Spanish descent.

The scenery along our journey has been nothing short of breathtaking and the smells have been gorgeous. We've passed by countless remote farms, with hundreds of woolly creatures dotting the landscape. Oh, the temptation to round them up, but alas, I am not permitted to indulge in such pursuits although it is my heritage. After all, both my parents were shepherds.

Progress aboard my long-kennel has been leisurely, as we've had to make frequent stops at the numerous swing bridges that pepper this farming region. These pauses afford my long-haired one and her friend Barbie, who join me on these towpath treks, the chance to catch up with my long-kennel. Some of the swing bridges halt road traffic to accommodate our passage. Mike takes great delight in operating these bridges, revelling in the sense of power it bestows. He dons a cap for these events!

At one swing bridge in Riddlesden, however, we encountered a malfunctioning mechanism that refused to yield. This is a recurring issue, and previous travellers have alerted the authorities about it.

Coincidentally, our very good friend Mr Toby Carvery happened to be in the vicinity, so we left my long-kennel to rendezvous with him for lunch while the problem was fixed.

As it turned out, lunch took place at this pub which is one of those food houses where we were compelled to sit outdoors due (would you believe it), to my presence. While my Pets indulged in substantial meals, I contented myself with a morsel of pork kindly offered by my bearded one. It had been thoroughly chewed, rendering it unsuitable for further human consumption, but I managed it gratefully.

After our meal, we returned to my long-kennel, to discover that the swing bridge had been repaired, it now swung, allowing us to continue our journey toward the remarkable Bingley 5 Rise locks. This magnificent lock structure, alongside its counterparts, the 3 and 2 Rise locks we will meet later gracefully lowers us by a staggering 100 feet.

Barry, the chief lock-keeper of 35 years, a man of few words, guided us through this procedure. This is a view looking back. Because all the locks are connected, with one lock filling  the next, these are called staircase locks.

The weather this afternoon has been delightful, although the day has been exhausting. We have settled for the night just west of Shipley, seeking respite from our endeavours. I confess to having lost count of the miles we have travelled, the tunnels we have passed, the bridges and aqueducts we have crossed and I am sure my bearded one will admonish me. But it is my intention to study the maps and calculate these figures for him when I have a chance. Suffice it to say that at this moment we are a little over halfway round our circular voyage in terms of miles. In terms of time, we have gone a little past the midway point. We will be spending some time travelling faster on rivers when we turn southwards on the mighty River Trent after visiting Leeds which is just around the corner.

Shipley to Rodley

As we approach Leeds, progress has been sluggish. Again it has been the abundance of swing bridges coupled with incessant rain that has impeded our journey. The rain has persisted throughout the day, dissuading me from venturing outdoors and thus preventing me from taking my Pets for their customary rambles. I've abstained from mischief and instead found peace in prolonged slumber. I like sleeping.

The day began with some promising glimpses of weak sunshine, and we eagerly anticipated a dry rendezvous in Rodley around lunchtime for a minor crew change. However, our aspirations were thwarted, and we only managed to reach Apperley, where a convenient marina wharf served as a suitable location for the crew transition amidst the downpour despite the rain. This proved to be a convenient area for loading and unloading. Today, we bade farewell to Mike and Barbie, who left us, only for a few days, and we welcomed two young humans of the grandchild variety, Emilio and Ruben, they are to accompany us on this leg of the journey into Leeds. This I have called a minor crew change, as they are minors. We anticipate Mike and Barbie's return after the young humans have been returned to their parents, these young are my Pets' children's children.

Tomorrow, our aim is to reach Leeds, where we face decisions regarding our onward journey. Plan A involves an adventurous route back to our base. My bearded one promises to provide further details later but suffice it to say that this plan may require additional muscle power for the challenges that lie ahead, assuming we are not hindered by any closures caused by the heavy rains. It appears we may embark on a memorable journey, traversing back over the Pennines - a feat that has been described as remarkable.

Despite the rain, I did venture out periodically today, braving the elements as we encountered another set of staircase locks. These locks provide an enjoyable diversion, and a boy must sometimes do what a boy has to do. These locks are similar and related to the ones we encountered yesterday at Bingley. This process involves utilising water from the top lock chamber to fill the lower chambers, an ingenious water conservation technique, although arguably unnecessary in our current circumstances. It has been a busy and wet day indeed and an early bed for all seemed a sensible proposition.

Leeds at Last!

What a delightful surprise awaited me this morning! As I opened my eyes, I was greeted by a magnificent expanse of blue sky adorned with plentiful sunshine. My bearded one announced at breakfast that we had triumphantly completed the 100-mile stretch of the Leeds & Liverpool Canal. My long-haired one expressed great joy at the prospect of drying all our wet and weathered towels, which have been used to rub me down when I become wet or to provide me with a comfortable resting place on the stern deck. They were thoroughly soaked, and their rejuvenation is most welcome. I will look forward to some warm bedding and an occasional rub down with a dry towel one of my favourite things.

Despite being less than 10 miles away from Leeds this morning, our journey from our mooring in Rodley required a full day's cruise. We encountered numerous swing bridges and several locks that demanded our attention before we could finally enter the vibrant city of Leeds.

I find this news splendid, as there will be ample opportunities for exploring. Our mooring in Leeds sounds exciting, it is situated at Clarence Dock, a delightful and secure location right in the heart of the city, adjacent to the Armoury Museum. I must confess, I am feeling weary. The boys have not stopped playing with me and it is absolutely exhausting.

We were very fortunate as we were able to join forces with another long-kennel named Zigane as we approached our first lock of the day. Zigane, a name that signifies 'gipsy' in both Hungarian and Italian, serves as the home to a kind and welcoming lady named Fran. While Fran has a bevy of visitors accompanying her on this journey, unfortunately, there are no fellow canines in sight. Nevertheless, the presence of my two small human companions onboard keeps me thoroughly engaged, and they truly tire me out! With the shared assistance we had, our journey now using double locks of course was not only entertaining but also remarkably trouble-free. Fran, an experienced traveller of these waters, having navigated this route numerous times and neighbouring routes near her own residence, imparted a wealth of knowledge to my bearded one regarding future options for our southward journey.

Our route plans remain somewhat uncertain as we await flood reports pertaining to potential river passages. Currently, it seems probable that we will adhere to our original plan of venturing south along the River Trent. This allows us the luxury of not having to rush and it grants us the opportunity to explore the captivating city of Leeds for maybe a day or two and also to include a visit to Lincoln in a week or so. We are pretty sure this is what we will do, it will be more leisurely assuming our river crossings will all be open.

Leeds, and It's Raining

It has been decided that we shall stay in Leeds, certainly for today, possibly tomorrow too, for several compelling reasons. Firstly, the weather is rather dreary for cruising, making it less than ideal. Secondly, Leeds beckons with its vast opportunities for exploration. I have never visited this city before and as far as I know, neither have my Pets, certainly not in my lifetime. Lastly, our current mooring in the city centre offers great conveniences, including access to electricity (my long-haired one wasted no time in getting the washing machine up and running) and the ability to replenish our water tanks. Although we can store over half a ton of water, with a full complement on board it is surprising how much we use, especially when the washing machine is active!

We find ourselves moored right alongside the Royal Armouries Museum, which means I shall remain on guard duty inside my long-kennel while the boys and their grandmother, my long-haired pet venture forth to investigate. Spot-on! They left me for a brief period phew, I had a quick nap but they have now returned, instructing me to stand sentry over my long-kennel, for they are heading back there once more! Oh, splendid!

Apparently, according to their accounts upon returning, the Royal Armouries Museum is indeed a fascinating place. They have attended several lectures and claim to have acquired a wealth of intriguing knowledge and a few souvenirs purchased with some pocket money that was a donation from my Pets.

Sadly, no one appears to have managed to grasp the art of turning off nature's obstinate cold water shower tap! I am not sure this is humanly possible. Consequently, my outings today have been quite limited. Yet, during a brief respite from the downpour, I seized the opportunity to teach the little ones how to engage in a spirited game of mouth-ball with me in an open space near the museum. We are playing by my rules. They are really quite good at football, I must admit, they managed to exhaust me once again! The smallest of the two was rather naughty, he kept kicking the ball into the water in a vain attempt to persuade me to follow it. I am too smart for that malarkey. My long-haired one showed him how to retrieve his ball with a net, all by himself. In the afternoon, while the rain persisted, we received a visit from an old friend, Jim, who had previously stayed with us in Spain. He came to see us at our mooring in Clarence Dock, and it was a pleasure to reunite with him. He shared a few beers with my bearded one and joined us all for supper.

Last Morning in Leeds

There are many advantages to a city mooring but from my point of view, there are also some small disadvantages. Allow me, if you will, to regale you with a brief tale: My bearded one needs his early morning saunter, as indeed do I. However, my own urgencies, being a dog, are perhaps sometimes a little more pressing. Clarence Dock, you see and the area all around is completely and utterly devoid of anything verdant. As we ventured forth on our exploratory sojourn this morning, traversing the roads, pathways and scent trails, it became evident that my astute bearded one, in his sagacity, was aware, bless him, of my pressing predicament. On rounding a corner, we were presented with a lone and genial member of the HM Constabulary.

"Good morning, officer," my bearded one announced in greeting, with a cheery smile, "can you please tell us where we can find some grass?"

To which the policeman, sternly but with a wry smile replied, "Well, sir, that depends, pray tell me, do you wish to smoke it or to mow it?"

In reply, my bearded one shook his head, and with a sad expression, gestured towards me, and stated, "He needs it to poop on." The affable constable appeared much amused, and with benevolence steered us towards some appropriate terrain. I was happy and my bearded one too was happy, as he likes, very much it seems, to collect and place my offerings in a little plastic bag that he always appears to have handy. This phenomenon, I confess, remains a mystery to my canine intellect, yet I strive to acquiesce to this peculiar human custom. I have never really understood it but I always try and oblige.

Chapter Six:
Leeds Lincoln

To Stanley Ferry

Bidding farewell to Leeds later that morning, our journey meandered onward towards the mighty River Trent. Our path intertwined with the Aire and Calder navigation, a venture demanding deft manoeuvres as we transitioned from canal to river, and vice versa. Oh, the tales I could share—evading unwelcome sandbanks required a nautical prowess of the highest order! Regrettably, our first rather spectacular attempt, during one of these tricky manoeuvres, found our progress abruptly halted by one of these sandy obstacles. A fortuitous passerby, guided by empathy, a length of rope and generous encouragement from my bearded one, assisted us in our removal from this quandary. The incident was met with reassuring words, "Occurs with regularity," he quipped.

We continued on our quite challenging way and after a while we came upon a serene mooring spot, offering respite amid the splendour of the countryside. During this intermission, my Pets and small humans embarked on a jaunt to Thwaites Mill, a revered destination in this area. Meanwhile, I assumed the noble post of guardian, vigilantly watching over our long-kennel. Thwaites Mill, a relic of the past now restored to its former glory, stands as a museum. A water-driven establishment dedicated to crafting putty among other things. A subject of renown locally, it apparently bears significance somehow in the art of glazing, whatever that might be, a matter that left my eyes a trifle glazed. I patiently listened to their narratives on their return and then we embarked on a spirited team football match though in my case, I actually caught and ran with the ball, they did the kicking, and they tried to catch me before I got the ball but then I fetched it and delivered it; they kicked it again. It is a great game, the rules are very simple, we all join in, it is one of my favourite things.

Once back on the Aire and Calder navigation, a sense of trepidation washed over us. Not only were we navigating rivers displaying cautionary 'orange' flow ratings, owing to unprecedented rainfall, but the locks themselves, when they appeared, which happily was not often, were colossal, designed to accommodate large commercial traffic, including the 600-ton barges that are common in these parts. They are mostly transporting sand. Fortunately, we encountered none of these vessels today. These massive locks can also service several water kennels and long-kennels like mine and bigger ones too, all at once. However, the absence of other long-kennels and humans to help and indeed the absence of anyone, including the official lock keepers, heightened our stress level somewhat, it reached a steady level number four on the long-haired one's anxiety scale, or so she stated.

Given the predominantly river-based nature of this part of our journey, opportunities for disembarking and strolling with my long-haired one were few and far between. Moreover, suitable mooring spots were scarce. Consequently, they relied on their trusty maps to locate a secure haven for the night. However, on this occasion, fortune did not smile upon us, the identified and chosen location we noticed, but only as we approached, was situated above an obviously damaged and thus non-operational flood lock, therefore out of our reach. Time was slipping away. Dusk was falling proportionate to our stress levels rising—to a number seven in the estimation of my long-haired one who reminded me that we had important cargo on board! This fuelled our need to alter our planned route a little and seek an alternative haven, with a certain degree of urgency!

Indeed, it was nearly dark when my bearded one, who seemed quite philosophical about it all (he is our intrepid captain), managed to secure us in a safe albeit not so salubrious refuge at Stanley Ferry. Finally, I was granted permission to frolic and play, while they tended to their own need which was, apparent to me, quite a thirst.

Stanley Ferry to Ferrybridge

The morning greeted us with a breathtaking sight—a clear blue sky and radiant sunshine. I took my bearded one for his morning stroll, we didn't venture far. Both he and I were still quite tired, thoroughly worn out by the boundless energy of those energetic young human boys. They certainly know how to tire us out!

If you've read my diary entry from yesterday, you'll understand that it was a long and somewhat stressful day. In addition, the rain persisted for a significant portion of our journey. In fact, I overheard them discussing the weather, noting that they could not recall a completely dry day save perhaps for one or two since starting this adventure a month ago, not that this mattered to them as a matter of fact, where we live in Spain they celebrate when it rains, they do not get nearly as much in a whole year as we have received through these last few weeks in England. I don't like rain but I do like having a rub down when I get wet, this is not so much for my benefit I think, it is that I am not really allowed in my long-kennel when I am too damp. However, I digress.

Summary: Last night, we found ourselves at Stanley Ferry, still on the Aire and Calder navigation. This was a small deviation from our original route due to our quest for secure mooring as it was getting dark. We arrived rather late into this area, and although suitable moorings were scarce and absent altogether on the river sections, my bearded one managed to find a safe and adequate haven for the night.

This morning, however, was another day and the world seemed transformed under the warm sunshine. We left early to retrace our steps with renewed spirits. Cruising along the expansive river sections, looking out for the 600-ton barges, proved to be a different but quite exhilarating experience. It was quite exciting when we saw a heavily laden one, well down in the water and fast approaching in the distance. There is a procedure. 'Get out of the way!' They do not take prisoners! Neither do they slow down or otherwise make any concessions for relatively small long-kennels, or any other craft. They are 'King of the River,' working barges couldn't care less about the wash they produce or indeed their enormous bow wave that they push along in front of their blunt noses.

We wasted no time and pulled over to our side of the river to give this oncoming behemoth all the room we could. As it passed us, it was impressive, we could see the enormous bow wave that would have surely overwhelmed us had we not taken action. These working barges are not to be disrespected. We bumped along over the wash when it had passed and we continued on our way. Thankfully, no more vessels crossed our path today. One advantage of deep river cruising is, as my bearded one explained exactly this, we too are able to drive my long-kennel at greater speed which is quite fun and a pleasant change for short periods and it does no harm to the banks. As my bearded one says it does our engine good to 'stretch its legs,' and to 'open the taps' a bit! Those mixed metaphors confused me.

Anyway, although the locks we encountered were of considerable size, they were electronically controlled and operated by traffic lights, sparing us from the need for excessive exertion. The larger of the two young humans displayed impressive skill in navigating the necessary button presses on these locks, climbing access ladders while assuming the role of our primary lock-keeper, as the officially employed ones were nowhere to be seen. My long-haired one claims she has grown many white hairs these last few days.

We encountered a slight delay at one lock, where a persistent flashing red light indicated dangerous river levels. 'Do not Proceed.' However, a phone call clarified that it should have displayed an amber light, signifying 'Proceed with Caution' thus allowing passage. Admittedly, this change disappointed me slightly, as I was rather enjoying a game with the two young ones, we were engrossed in a spirited game of mouth-ball, while we awaited the alteration of the lights and I was winning.

Our next stop was in the district of Castleford, coinciding perfectly with the onset of a massive rainfall. Unfortunately, even sunshine would have done little to improve the waterfront area, which appeared desolate and forlorn. The water taps that we desperately needed were vandalised, and there was no fuel at all available, both of these supplies were becoming rather necessary. The visitor moorings held little appeal, lacking any facilities whatsoever. It was a disheartening sight, considering it was once, but a few years ago, a thriving area.

However, my bearded one managed to locate Mr John Smith, again, he seemed like a familiar friend and we enjoyed refreshments and shared a pizza at the Griffin, quite a pleasant human food house, I was welcomed under their table in a special outside covered area. Especially for folk like me that have human companions.

Moving onward, we reached Ferrybridge, only to discover that no visitor moorings at all were available. Fortunately, a generous fellow long-kennel owner graciously invited us to moor alongside him. We accepted the kind offer, as we had arranged to reunite the two young humans with their parents in this vicinity. The Golden Lion, a short walk from this mooring, served as our meeting point. Interestingly, John Smith seemed to be a regular here too. He gets about!

Our rendezvous at The Golden Lion took place in the presence of a rather intimidating landlord. Towering at nearly 7 feet, topped by a shiny shaved head, sporting a six-inch-long goatee beard, and covered in a myriad of tattoos across a massive black vested upper torso of rippling muscles, he exuded an air of authority. We imagined he encountered few issues with his patrons. I in particular received a very warm welcome and a pat on my head, which we have discovered, in this region, is not always so gently done. When my bearded one asked this giant, "Can we eat with our dog under the table?"

He replied gruffly, "No," adding, "We would prefer you to sit—at the table!" In the event they obeyed, I took up my position as usual and we all had an enjoyable stay. When the boys' daddy arrived, we gratefully delivered our two young charges back to him and returned to our long-kennel utterly exhausted. Sleep swiftly enveloped us.

Ferrybridge to Junction Canal

With our moorings at Ferrybridge behind us, we set off on our journey today. Our primary mission was to collect Mike for yet another return visit, he is to be joining us for the upcoming adventure on the mighty Trent in a couple of days' time. This is a little daunting, although we have had a taste of rivers recently, this is a big wide one. It is fair to say, we are more at home on the tranquil, tideless and gentle waters of our beloved canals.

Our rendezvous point was the Morrisons supermarket in Knottingley, just a few miles away. Mike's wife, our friend Barbie, kindly drove him to us. We met and loaded our friend on board along with provisions at an old quarry wharf nearby since convenient boarding areas were scarce. Remarkably, the weather remains favourable, with no signs of rain. If we manage to make it through the day without a single drop, it will be noteworthy indeed!

Our voyage along the Aire and Calder navigation proved to be both intriguing and distinct in many ways from the canals we are accustomed to down south. The landscape stretched out flat before us, with the occasional interruption of wind farms and nests of cooling towers on the horizon.

Navigating the working rivers, although they were hardly busy, was an exciting experience.

Interestingly, the locks along our route, although sparse in number, were of considerable size and electrically operated. I took the opportunity to disembark at these locks where I could and indulge in a good sniff around. However, I couldn't help but notice the absence of both my fellow canines, their human counterparts and indeed other long-kennels for that matter. These waterways seemed sparsely travelled by pleasure craft. During our journey, we paused for a picnic, a first on this holiday. A special table was conveniently stationed on the towpath for us. The weather remained mild, contributing to a pleasant interlude. I like picnics best when they spread all the food out on a rug on the floor. One of my favourite things.

In the afternoon, we joined The New Junction Canal. Here is a bit of technical information that might be of interest: Apart from the Manchester Ship Canal, a major project which was constructed for ocean-going vessels connecting Manchester with the Irish Sea, circa 1895, The Junction Cut as it is also known was the final canal to be constructed in England. It stretches in a perfectly straight line for over five miles. It connects the Aire and Calder navigation with the Sheffield and South Yorkshire Navigation It was opened in 1839. This canal allowed for more direct and improved navigation between these two larger systems. It played a big role in enhancing transportation and trade in the area back in the heyday of canals in the 19th century.

As evening approached, we made the decision to halt our progress and settle halfway along this Junction Cut. The area provided ample space for quiet play and exercise and a quiet and pleasant mooring. Before settling down for supper and succumbing to sleep, I treated my long-haired one to a lovely extended walk along this dead straight and serene scent trail, they call a towpath.

Junction Canal to Keadby

Today we set our sights on Keadby, this is where The Sheffield and South Yorkshire Navigation joins the River Trent. This marks our final destination for the day. Tomorrow, at 7:00 am, we are booked in and will be locking through and down onto the River Trent taking advantage of the flowing ebb tide to assist us upstream for the start of our southward journey in the direction of Nottingham. Today promises to be sunny and mild, much like yesterday. Remarkably, it just might be more or less our second completely dry day on this adventure!

Before starting on this last stretch, we enjoyed a pleasant stroll, taking in the new sights and smells of our surroundings. Our mooring on the Junction Canal, nestling in the middle of a remote and sparsely populated area, provided a tranquil start to the day. To fortify ourselves for the journey ahead, we indulged in a nourishing breakfast. I say we, actually, my bearded one and his friend Mike enjoyed a full English, whatever that is, my long-haired one had something colourfully fruity being a vegetarian but which I did not think was very appetising, the bacon smelled good, I contented myself with the all-too-familiar fare of dried biscuits alas, not the most exciting culinary experience for a canine of my status I am beginning to think.

The journey itself was devoid of significant challenges or stress, save for the frequent encounters with swing bridges. For me, it meant a familiar routine of hopping off the long-kennel and back on (on the command Okay) as my Pets skilfully navigated our long-kennel along the dead straight canal. This does not seem too onerous to me. The landscape that unfolded before us was strikingly flat, interrupted only by the imposing presence of numerous wind turbines, an aspect that seemed to evoke a mixed response from my bearded one. I think he thinks they are not very pretty. I suspect they are quite useful as a power source but what do I know, I am a dog.

We made a stop for lunch in a small settlement called Thorne. There, we discovered one surviving pub, another derelict, and a couple of boatyards. While my bearded one and his friend Mike managed the long-kennel, preparing her for her river adventure, my refreshed long-haired one took the opportunity to enjoy a leisurely amble with me for nearly an hour. Occasional signs of life punctuated the otherwise serene surroundings, with farms dotting the landscape. We also encountered a stretch of canal where at least a hundred fishermen had congregated, seemingly participating in a fishing competition. Each angler was regimentally spaced along the canal bank as far as my eyes could see. I have to say, I was impressed by their behaviour.

As we gently cruised along the line, it was like a ceremony. Each fisherman in turn, as we passed by, raised his rod, in a respectful salute, I suppose. They were very solemn, not one of them spoke or smiled, as soon as we had passed each one then lowered his rod ceremoniously back to the water Not one made eye contact. In fact, no eyes ever left the water. I suspect this is highly correct and respectful behaviour shown by fishermen to long-kennels of our status as they pass by.

Upon reaching the grand finale of today's journey, Keadby Lock, the evening turned out to be quite interesting. With my long-kennel moored up in preparation for tomorrow's exploits. My Pets all sat around having a discussion about the next day's plan, sharing a well-earned libation of gin and tonic. Suddenly, my Pets and their friends espied across the water an antique-looking water kennel of substantial proportions. Here was an antique vessel named SpiderT, that captured my bearded one's particular admiration. It piqued his curiosity to such an extent that he, along with his friend Mike and my long-haired one, managed an invitation from the owner for a personal and exclusive tour of this splendid old sailing vessel. I wasn't included. They all returned to my long-kennel well impressed, remarking that she was lovely.

Her name is as peculiar as her design, SpiderT is much heavier, wider, and older than my long-kennel. She weighs 200 tons and is a beautifully restored Humber Sloop, the survivor of just two of this design. She has a length of 62 feet and was launched in 1926. She holds an interesting history. She is based at Keadby Lock and is a popular tourist attraction, and is available for charter. The small town of Keadby holds little else of notable distinction, save for its juncture with the venerable River Trent, the abandonment of its two pubs casting a sombre shadow over the place. We position ourselves for the adventure in the morning and as it is an early start we all have an early night!

Onto The River Trent

It was early but oh, what a splendid morning it was! The sun greeted us as it peeped above the horizon, promising us a beautiful day—a potential run of three consecutive days of fine weather! Well, we are now in September. My bearded one roused me from my slumber for a quick dawn patrol. It was very early and I had overslept. There was a bit of activity around and an awful lot of excitement and I even had the pleasure of playing for a short while with a fellow companion—a member of an unknown tribe. I think she was, of mixed lineage but she was rather pretty and she was sprightly, about nine months old, and despite my best efforts, I couldn't help but emerge victorious in our playful chase games.

As the time for our departure grew near, I reluctantly endured the process of getting dressed for our river journey: O boy, did my bum look big in that! It is not worth recording, I was dressed in a really bulky harness-type bra thingy that would float even with two of me inside it. In the event that I was to have another aquatic misadventure, there would be no chance of swimming. I would just bob up and down. Anyway, I am going to make damn sure it does not serve its purpose. I will make sure I do not fall into the river. I could end up anywhere!

At precisely 7:00 am, a friendly lock-keeper paid a visit to each of us four similar-sized long-kennels in waiting. He assigned us the order in which we were to enter his lock. As fate would have it, three of us—similar in size—entered the lock first, all line abreast. There was a remarkable covering of thick algae on the water in the lock which I thought was grass. Fortunately, though tempted, I was unable to test this, I was just curious. When some other long-kennels of various shapes and sizes were added and stationed behind us, we were all lowered down ready to join the river. Then, the gates slowly opened to reveal the mighty River Trent rushing past…

We left one at a time, we were first out and this was daunting but a delightful experience, standing on the aft deck

alongside my Pets as my bearded one skilfully manoeuvred my long-kennel out into the swiftly flowing river. With the helm over to starboard, we embraced the rush of uncontrolled momentum, racing along with the tide at what appeared to be an astonishing speed that we maintained for nearly 30 miles over the next three hours or so. It was an exhilarating ride, filled with twists and turns—a white-knuckle experience, or so my bearded one claims. Well, a little exaggeration but I like to add a bit of drama to the tale. There was not a lot to report from the passing scenery, it was expansive and empty with magnificent skies rising from flat horizons interrupted only by the occasional clutch of cooling towers or remote farm buildings.

Our plan, and in fact our first opportunity to do so, is to leave the river when we arrive at Torksey and join the Fossdyke Navigation. to take us on to Lincoln. After a little more than three hours of this thrilling white-knuckle ride, we were ready for this change of pace. Although the tide had slackened a little as we left the Trent, my bearded one by skilful manoeuvring, swung a wide turn to port and entered the calm waters of this ancient Roman canal, without hitting anything! The Fossdyke as it is called is the first man-made waterway in England as opposed to the last one mentioned yesterday. This one was constructed by The Romans to connect the City of Lincoln with the River Trent an awful long time ago even in human years, supposedly in about 58 AD.

It was quiet again and we found the perfect spot for a late lunch and, for me, a much-needed bathroom break. I know it is not their fault, they could not have stopped anywhere anyway but they just might forget that they have a bathroom onboard, I am relegated to finding one on land, preferably grass (as you may have noted from my visit to Leeds) for such needs. Anyway, I was much relieved. We made a stop at the village of Saxilby, halfway to Lincoln.

Regrettably, signs of economic downturn were evident here as well, if my bearded one's theory about pubs being an economic barometer holds any truth. One pub did not offer food and the other did not offer anything at all. It was closed, boarded up, shut, abandoned! However, we were directed to a municipal sports centre, where we discovered an astonishing spread of culinary surprises, Mr Wadworth was in residence!

I remember him from when I was younger. I got a pig's ear treat, well I buried that!

Following our lunch stop, I had the opportunity for a satisfying romp, the sprawling playing fields provided ample space for me to stretch my legs with my long-haired one and play a version of mouth-ball. The rules are very simple she kicks the ball, I catch it, if I can or fetch it back and drop it at her feet to be kicked again and so it goes on. I can do this for hours, I just love her expression of joy as I keep returning the ball to her. It clearly gives her so much pleasure, it is so gratifying and it makes all my efforts seem worthwhile.

Onward we travelled to Lincoln, enjoying the continued warmth and loveliness of the day. I happily settled down on the aft deck while my bearded one with his friend Mike skilfully guided my long-kennel into the heart of Lincoln City. An impressive ride. Tomorrow, we will embark on our exploration of this historic place. But for now, we are all taking a well-deserved rest, we have travelled many miles today.

Lincoln City

Ah, what a delightful morning it was! The sun's golden rays entered my bedroom through the porthole, gently awakening me from my slumber. I must say, I do like my bedroom atop the engine of my long-kennel, as I have told you before, it is lovely and warm for me when I go to bed on the cooler nights which are now becoming evident.

Today, our plans are to explore the charming city of Lincoln—a day filled with plenty of walking, which happens to be one of my favourite things. As the city unfolded before us, I couldn't help but bask in the magic atmosphere that enveloped us. The sight of the majestic Cathedral perched atop the hill greeted our eyes, and we set off on a stroll up Steep Street an aptly named thoroughfare, I had to lend a paw to assist my bearded one, he made several stops as we climbed, he said to admire the view.

Eventually, we arrived at the Cathedral and discovered the nearby castle as well as the fact that I was denied entry.

However, humans were permitted inside, this was expected and my bearded one kindly volunteered to keep me company, while we sat outside at a nearby pub. He did some sketching as my long-haired pet and our friend Mike delved into the secrets of the Magna Carta, I contented myself with watching the world go by from our vantage point from where later we had a grandstand view of the graduation ceremony for bright young humans from Lincoln University. It was indeed a splendid sight to see all these young humans wearing funny square hats with colourful silk adornments to their long robes parading the ancient streets, it was just like a grand fashion show.

After the graduation proceedings concluded, we strolled back down Steep Street towards the canal basin. There, my Pets and Mike enjoyed a meal at a floating restaurant aptly called 'The Barge,' while I found solace under the table, sadly without any lunch. I wasn't hungry anyway.

In the afternoon, while my long-haired one took care of provisioning—ensuring I had a fresh supply of Chappie and biscuits—my bearded one and his friend Mike took it upon themselves to wash and polish one side of my long-kennel, the side they were unable to reach a few days ago. So now they feel my long-kennel can show the world how to keep things shipshape!

Once we regrouped, we set off on our cruise back to Saxilby, where we plan to spend the night in preparation for our return and departure onto and onward up the quieter but still mighty River Trent tomorrow.

Chapter Seven:
Lincoln Lichfield

On The Trent to Newark

My bearded one, if you remember in his wisdom and kindness, purchased a pig's ear as a special treat for me when we visited Saxilby on our way to Lincoln a couple of days ago. I was very grateful, but my natural instinct overtook me and led me to bury it pretty well immediately. This was much to his dismay at the time, as he said it was very expensive. This morning, on our return to Saxilby after our stay in Lincoln, as I ventured out to stretch my legs, I knew exactly where it was. I had not forgotten it. I dug up the buried treasure and happily devoured it. I can tell you it had vastly improved in flavour for its internment. Oh, the simple pleasures.

There was no great hurry this morning, ah, the fifth day of summer—or so it seemed—as we prepared for our departure from Saxilby. The sun beamed down upon us, and the joyful melodies of birds filled the air, setting the stage for a delightful day ahead. Just as a matter of interest, today is the 35th day of our voyage since we started from Kings Bromley. Today, we had an appointment with a lock but we had plenty of time. We had time for a nourishing breakfast and a final frolic plus my bearded one's walkabout all before he untied my trusty long-kennel, and we set off on our potter back to

Torksey, where we would rejoin the River Trent. This was our appointment with Mr Nice Lock-keeper, timed to catch the turning tide from flow to ebb to ease our ascent to Newark.

By noon, we had passed through the lock. The pace was brisk, with no time for pausing, and it was three hours later when we reached the end of the tidal Trent at Cromwell Lock. At this point, I wasn't able to disembark, as the lock was quite a substantial size, accommodating not only us but four other long-kennels. It took another hour and a half before we finally arrived at King's Marina, where a reserved berth awaited us for the night.

Once my bearded one had moored us at our allocated mooring B 10, I was finally granted the 'Okay' word to step off and, hooray, I discovered a patch of vegetation nearby. Little did I know at the time, it was actually a long-kennel's herb garden—Oops! I suppose I wasn't supposed to use it for my purposes, but in the moment, it brought me great relief. My Pets seemed quite philosophical, they like to collect my offerings. They carry a little plastic bag around with them for these occasional happenings.

We ventured out to explore the charming town of Newark, paying visits to the odd human watering hole and food house and enjoying long walks. They decided to have supper by the river at Pizza Express, while I contented myself by resting beneath their table, and was graciously offered a bucket of water—much appreciated. The views along the riverside were quite stunning.

Newark

Oh, the excitement is palpable today! My dear friend Josh is coming to visit me all the way from Greenwich. Josh is a proud member of the Spaniel tribe and he used to have a long-kennel like mine. His Pets, Jackie and Brendan, are friends of my Pets.

Today, we bid farewell to Mike, who has been a tremendous help to my bearded one throughout our journey from Yorkshire. His assistance has been invaluable, and we shall miss his company.

Now, let me tell you about the weather. It appears that today may well be our sixth day of summer mostly sunny, albeit with a bit of wind and a hint of coolness. But, it remains dry, allowing us to venture out and enjoy the day.

Josh arrived with his Pets around midday, accompanied by their friend Sarah, who happens to reside here in Newark. We all excitedly climbed aboard my trusty long-kennel for a delightful cruise taking us to a restaurant not far away for lunch (for them). We travelled against a strong wind and current for over two hours, braving the elements to reach our destination: The Boathouse, a charming human eatery in Farndon. From what I gathered from their conversations, they had a splendid meal. Josh and I managed to score a few scraps and a piece of bread—a delightful treat for us loyal and loving four-legged companions. As there is a sizeable lock situated in the heart of Newark, which we must pass through before 4:45 p.m., we had to begin our return journey promptly after lunch. Thankfully, the wind and current were in our favour this time, aiding our progress, and we successfully navigated the lock in good time.

Later in the evening, Sarah graciously extended an invitation for them to join her for supper at her house. Unfortunately, I was not included in the gathering. However, I relished the opportunity to rest and dutifully guard the long-kennel. Besides, I had already enjoyed my serving of chappie and biscuits. Josh, being a bit younger and filled with boundless energy, surely had a grand time.

They said goodbye to our friends and Josh. It was quite late when they arrived back at my long-kennel. They had their customary cocoa and I had their biscuit and we went to bed.

Newark to Hazelford Island

Ah, how we adore this town! Newark has captured our hearts, and we've decided to extend our stay for another day before setting off later this afternoon. It's a picturesque place, brimming with fascinating attractions, delightful strolls, and charming parks. This morning, I accompanied my bearded one on his walk in the park by the castle, merrily fetching balls which he launched with my trusty ball launcher, it's a favourite pastime of his. Certainly one of my favourite things. He enjoys it, he is always so pleased when I bring the ball back, bless him. Meanwhile, my long-haired one busied herself with provisioning for the next leg of our journey. She cannot launch the ball quite as far as my bearded one can.

Today, we have the pleasure of being joined by our dear friends Lawson and Jan. They reside in Cambridgeshire but also, have a house near us in Vinuela, Spain. The weather today is hot and sunny—a true testament to the seventh day of summer. We've been blessed with an entire week of sunshine, not a drop of rain!

Lawson and Jan arrived bearing gifts, lunch for them all and a delightful treat for me. A bone-shaped biscuit. We savoured our meal together, enjoying each other's company and preparing for our departure. Given the glorious weather and the fact that it is the weekend, we anticipate that moorings along the river, which are already scarce, will be even more challenging to find today.

Setting sail from Newark, we bade the town farewell and set our sights on Farndon, hoping to secure a mooring spot for the night. Alas, luck was not on our side, as there was no available space. Undeterred, we pressed on to the next potential mooring, only to find it too was full and in any case quite difficult for a dog like me to disembark. The walls towered 20 feet high, rendering it impossible for me to set my paw on solid ground. We had no other choice but to continue our journey. When we arrived at Hazelford Lock, my bearded one showcased his remarkable manoeuvring skills, expertly mooring my long-kennel in a space barely six inches longer than our 58-foot length.

Despite the swift current and the towering 10-foot wall, he triumphed. However, I encountered the same predicament—unscalable walls that stood high above my kennel's roof. I was unceremoniously carried off.

Undeterred by these challenges, we started on a delightful exploration around the island, discovering its unique charm. It turns out, Hazelford is an island separated by two weirs with plenty of rabbits frolicking about—an absolute playground for me! Though I haven't caught one yet, I'm determined and ever hopeful. I will have a go in the morning.

Rabbit Island

Another lovely morning and greetings from this unique confluence! At Hazelford Lock, the river branches off, creating two arms of the mighty Trent. The presence of weirs on either side has blessed us with a magnificent island mooring. This, my bearded one discovered and negotiated to before breakfast this morning. I can get on and off at this one! We plan to stay for a few hours. I've dubbed it 'Rabbit Island' due to the abundance of large rabbits that playfully dart in and out of the bramble bushes, ever taunting me.

My bearded one and I embarked on an exciting roam along the picturesque paths, but alas, I have yet to catch one of these elusive creatures. They are quite quick but are not quite as challenging as squirrels, they can't climb trees apparently, I keep trying, I will catch one, hope springs eternal!

Today's weather is nothing short of exquisite—clear skies and a radiant sun that warms both body and soul. We are not in a hurry today, our plan for the evening is to rendezvous with my bearded one's eldest son James and his family at the Ferry Boat at Stoke Bardolf. To reach this charming establishment, we'll navigate a couple of locks this afternoon and cover a few pleasant miles, the calm waters of the River Trent offer the perfect conditions for a leisurely cruise—it truly feels like the epitome of summer.

As we arrived at the pub, much to our delight and indeed our surprise, a mooring spot awaited our arrival. Despite the early hour, we decided to seize this stroke of luck and remain here for the rest of the day and evening—at least! While my humans enjoyed a light lunch inside the pub (I, savoured a few delectable prawn heads), we spent the afternoon basking in the tranquillity of the river's edge. I even struck up a sort of respectful friendship with the graceful swans, observing their elegant movements with great interest. I am not convinced they thought me so graceful.

Meanwhile, my bearded one and my long-haired one engaged in the art of painting—a pursuit that brings them joy and relaxation. Amidst our leisurely activities, we witnessed a peculiar sight—a man swimming on his back across the river while precariously balancing four ice cream cornets on his chest. Additionally, we bore witness to a rather comical incident involving a gentleman who, while mooring his boat, experienced an unscheduled plunge into the water. And let us not forget the swans, marching with apparent determination after a lady clutching a bag of bread, a scene that elicited both curiosity and amusement.

Later in the day, I embarked on a leisurely stroll with my Pets and friends, through a serene field populated by contented cows. I must admit, on this occasion, they were still munching away, I maintained impeccable conduct. Allow me to share with you what happened next. It was on this country ramble that we stumbled upon a modest group of shops. At this point, my long-haired one decided that we had a need to do a small food shop. Regrettably, I am denied entry to these establishments. My bearded one nobly volunteered to remain by my side and so, we sat ourselves comfortably upon a convenient bench outside, bathed in the warm late summer sunshine. He promised to keep an eye on me.

In truth, however, he succumbed to closing both of them, he was soon deep in slumber! Feeling a trifle bored, and with my discerning nose tempting me along the scent trail of my long-haired one, I drifted a little away and I was surprised when suddenly, a big glass door magically slid open before me, and I immediately found myself inside a very large room surrounded with nothing but food, arranged in meticulous rows, and with many humans manoeuvring trolleys laden with the stuff.

Wow! If you have never been to a supermarket, you must go, they are nothing short of wondrous. Inside, I received many kind greetings and much admiration. I had of course completely forgotten my original mission of locating my long-haired one, I was so enjoying this attention and this new experience. Then, out of nowhere appeared a man in a white coat. I know he was the owner, it was Mr Tesco himself! He had his name displayed on his coat with a short message 'Every Little Helps.' He was very nice, he spoke kindly to me as he fastened me with a lead and escorted me outdoors. My now awake and alert bearded one greeted us, for he had been anxiously searching for me. He and Mr Tesco engaged in a genial conversation and thus we were reunited, much to his relief. Upon her return, my long-haired one remained blissfully unaware of the grand adventure that had transpired in her absence.

My bearded one's son James rang to inform us that he would be unable to join us this evening. He found himself engrossed in a harvest, and with the weather being exceptionally fine, he expected to work until the stroke of midnight. Ah, the life of a farmer! We had a pleasant evening ourselves and after a fine supper went soundly to sleep.

Ferry Boat to Nottingham

Greetings from another day of glorious sunshine! The sky is a seamless expanse of blue, and the temperature is already soaring. It's the ninth consecutive day of no rain, with not even a whisper of wind. The river lies calm, resembling a serene millpond. I've just returned from taking my bearded one for his morning amble, and the heat is already palpable. Today promises to reach a scorching 26 degrees. A true summer's day.

Leaving our very pleasant mooring at the Ferry Boat, with its excellent amenities, is not easy. I have thoroughly enjoyed my time here delighting in ample supplies of goose droppings, one of my favourite things, taunting swans, chasing ducks, and goading geese. And of course, there were plenty of my fellow canines to engage with in playful escapades. It has been an idyllic respite. One of my best days.

Last night, my Pets enjoyed a satisfying supper at the pub—they told me. Though their family couldn't join them, they seemed content, muttering about some sort of special offer—two for ten, or something, a bit beyond my mathematical understanding.

As for me, my duty was to guard the kennel, which conveniently allowed me to catch up on some well-deserved rest. Fortunately, they don't mind me sleeping on duty. I am a very light sleeper and can be instantly alert and ever watchful.

As the sun began to rise in the morning sky, we set forth on our journey. Our first stop was Stoke Lock, followed by Holme Lock, where we decided to replenish our freshwater supply. The tap here, it had been reported, was disappointingly slow, it was going to take at least an hour to fill our tank and so we took advantage of our arrival at The National Water Sports Centre to enjoy the spectacle—a sight to behold.

This untamed stretch of the Trent, although man-made, transformed into a colossal whitewater park. We settled ourselves on a rug to watch and we marvelled at kayakers bouncing along the tumultuous waves, at times disappearing only to re-emerge yards downstream. Large inflatable rafts careened through the rapids, filled with eight athletic youngsters engaged in what seemed like a mad, exhilarating race, egged on by a chorus of boisterous spectators. The sight was so enticing that I longed to join in the merriment, but alas, I was attached to my long-haired one to ensure her safety. Actually, on reflection, water and I do not get on well.

After indulging in a delightful lunch, we consumed from our rug, a real picnic and with our water supply replenished we continued our journey towards Nottingham. Just around a bend in the river, we found ourselves in the middle of a regatta of sailing dinghies. They zigzagged haphazardly, completely unaware of the fifteen-ton kennel, with my bearded one at the helm, relentlessly approaching. After skilfully manoeuvring through this maze of chaos, we were soon confronted by a flotilla of canoes spanning the width of the river on the next bend. Their arrangement was far from disciplined, displaying varying degrees of inexperience. Miraculously, we managed to navigate through without sinking, not even one of them.

As we bade adieu to the river and returned into the tranquil, canalised section of the Trent, we sailed past notable landmarks such as Trent Bridge, Nottingham Forest, and Notts County football grounds—all within half a mile's reach. I love football! We then traversed a slightly rundown stretch of the city for a couple of miles before gradually transitioning into a more picturesque landscape. Leisure boaters and occasionally grumpy fishermen became more prevalent as we approached Beeston Lock—our haven for the night. Tomorrow, we shall once again, for a short while, rejoin the flowing embrace of the river.

Beeston to Shardlow

As the drought conditions persisted, there was just a hint in the overcast morning sky, of the possibility of approaching rain. The temperature had dropped about 10 degrees, bringing some relief from the heat. After my breakfast, I dutifully took my bearded one for his early morning walkabout while it was still dry and then we set sail and embarked on our journey from Beeston Lock.

Our cruise this morning led us through Trent-lock and back to the familiar embrace of the River Trent for just a couple more hours. The rain had still not appeared.

Upon reaching Sawley, we rejoined our beloved and familiar Trent and Mersey canal, our cherished home turf if indeed I can refer to a canal this way. There was a certain comfort in these familiar waters, especially for the towpath, my special scent trail, as this provided ample walking and running and exploration opportunities for me that were scarce on some of our recent days on the river.

Lunchtime found us at Shardlow, where we halted our journey to savour a pleasant interlude at The Malt Shovel. Mr Pedigree lives here and his ale flowed smoothly, and the aroma of a homemade meat pie wafted tantalisingly in the air.

Naturally, I, being only a keen observer from under the table, had no chance to partake in such delights.

Though the sky remained overcast, the threat of rain seemed to dissipate, happily leaving the drought to persist. As we resumed our travels after lunch, the sun managed to peek through the clouds, bidding us farewell on our onward journey.

For a change of scenery, we decided to moor up in the countryside, far away from the bustle of civilisation, surrounded by recently harvested fields. I took my long-haired one for a delightful early evening stroll, albeit with a minor mishap on our return. While attempting to drink from the canal, I lost my balance and ended up with a bit more than a wet bottom. My owners, preoccupied with their own liquid needs, remained oblivious to my little escapade until I joined them, wet and without ceremony upon the foredeck, They were, up to this point, sitting there enjoying their own refreshing gin and tonic all dressed up to go out for the evening. I think my long-haired one decided to change clothes while I got a lovely rub down. We are all going out to meet with some old friends who live nearby.

I felt honoured as I had been extended an invitation, these friends, Graeme and Angie, who also shared close amiable ties with Lawson and his wife Jan, exhibited the utmost kindness towards me. On our visit to their house, they graciously guided me through their meticulously tended garden, an array of magnificent and diverse plants captivating the senses. A plan was forming: when they retreated indoors, I was invited but I opted to remain among the verdant sanctuary, for I had spied, and really wanted to investigate further, that many of their plants had been graced with the wondrous dressing of what I now know was bone meal. I saw this as irresistible. A variety of flora dressed in this stuff was indeed contained in decorative food bowls presented at exactly the right height. I thought to myself—*How generous!* Now, I had never in my life seen or tasted this peculiar substance before but I must confess that the bouquet was delightful, a gustatory revelation almost beyond compare. I sampled a bit with an enthusiastic lick and perhaps, forgetting my manners, cleared the lot. I am not sure anyone noticed. When we were back on board my long-kennel, I went straight to bed, I was feeling very happy and just a little tired.

Off to Burton

It is very odd, I had some weird dreams last night and I cannot remember the details but O boy, were they weird, this morning, as I took my bearded one and his friend Lawson for their early morning exploration, I felt slightly strange. The world looked so bright. I saw everything in colour, I am not supposed to be able to do that. I just wonder about my unexpected gastronomic experience of last night. The treat was so generously given to me by my new good friend Graeme.

Continuing our journey as we meander through the borders of Derbyshire and into Staffordshire, on the last leg of this adventure the landscape remains largely unchanged. There are hardly any signs of human or animal habitation, just neatly cropped fields and safely stored harvests being the dominant features. Apart from the occasional duck, there seems to be a dearth of creatures for me to chase or play with. Nevertheless, it is excellent terrain exploring the long scent trails, and I managed to cover a mile or two alongside my long-haired one, complemented by the frequent presence of locks. I enjoy helping at these, in an advisory capacity, I usually get some company and admiration doing so and often some four-legged friends to sniff and play with.

Today, the wind proves a bit forceful and capricious. Manoeuvring through tight spaces with currents and crosswinds becomes somewhat unpredictable when you have a 58-foot floating windbreak like our long-kennel. So my bearded one mutters as he struggles at the helm along some of the river sections. Such was our predicament today that we found it prudent to slow our forward motion with the assistance of a rope. This resulted in a somewhat abrupt and rather unintended stop that caused my kennel to tilt a little, momentarily, unsettling a few unsecured objects. Today, it happened to be two soup bowls, three dinner plates, and a mug. Fortunately, my trusty tin bowl remained intact. My long-haired one was not amused.

Given the sunny and dry weather, albeit with a forecast of rain tomorrow, my bearded one and his friend Lawson decided it best to forgo a leisurely sit-down lunch and keep going managing with a sandwich and soup, taken from the surviving crockery, and aim to moor on the outskirts of Burton, rather than in the town itself. They sought a peaceful and secure overnight mooring.

As luck would have it, we discovered a delightful spot at Branston, just outside Burton-on-Trent, nestled beside a water park. This location promises ample opportunities for further exploration with my Pets and their companions. Fortuitously, adjacent to our mooring spot stands a pub named The Bridge, which happens to be the home of Marston Brewery. I can only assume that Mr Pedigree awaits within its walls. My Pets and their companions Lawson and Jan plan to visit him for their evening meal. Sadly, we say goodbye to Lawson and Jan, my Pets' friends for these last few days, they are to return to their home tonight after supper. They have their own canine family waiting there.

Almost Home

Dear diary, just a short weather report, There has been just a little rain overnight but it departed, leaving behind a sunlit day. We had a gentle cruise to Fradley Junction this morning where we stopped for breakfast but, before this, I accompanied my bearded one on his early morning amble around the beautiful and impressive water park in Fradley. This place is truly magnificent, filled with lively squirrels that continuously elude my grasp. Of course, you know that they can climb trees, but I can't, alas, I have given up on my pursuit of the ducks, for they possess remarkable skills.

Not only can they gracefully swim (water does not befriend me), but they can also run, flap, jump, and remain airborne—a most extraordinary feat.

Today marks our final stretch, a mere four locks and a pawful of miles from King's Bromley, where my long-kennel resides while we are in Spain. Farewells shall be bittersweet, for I have had such a wonderful time, surrounded by dear human friends old and new, I have met many new fellow canine friends. Although most of them communicated in English, our interactions were nothing short of splendid.

Nonetheless, today brings another visitor to accompany us on this last leg of our journey. It is my bearded one's son-in-law's father, John who resides not far away. He joined us shortly after 10:00 am, for a cruise back to our base and after indulging in some coffee and a spot of shopping, we embarked on our way.

However, disaster struck at our second lock, with just two more remaining. I encountered a spirited and amiable young new friend from the Jack Russell tribe, and our playful game swiftly escalated into a thrilling chase. All was going splendidly well, and in my favour until…I found myself sprinting across the grass, aiming to take a shortcut onto the bridge that spanned the lock's exit. To my dismay, a recently installed barrier obstructed my intended landing stage, supposedly erected for 'elf and safety' purposes. At my height, it abruptly and dangerously arrested my progress. I had no chance to land safely. I crashed into the barrier, somersaulting over the edge from a height of approximately 13 feet above the canal. My four legs scrambled desperately to save me but to no avail. At that precise moment, a kennel similar to mine was exiting the lock (while my own kennel patiently waited to enter).

I plummeted about eight feet before colliding with its front deck, with a resounding thud. I bounced off and fell another five feet into the water. Ugh! This was directly in front of the advancing kennel, which mercifully managed to avoid me and come to a halt. Gasping for air, I instinctively began swimming, although I am not good at it and do not like it and my body ached somewhat. Reaching the side, a kind gentleman pulled me out onto the grassy bank. Fear gripped me, and the same sentiment echoed through my Pets, they truly believed this was the end. I, too, feared the worst.

This is the lock that I will always remember. Drawn just before my accident. However, a happy ending awaited me. Following a thorough checkover by my concerned Pets, some rest and gentle examination from other caring humans, it was determined that no bones were broken and no serious harm had befallen me. It was likely that I was only bruised and expected to feel rather sorry for myself for a while. But, I was young and strong. Treats were offered, and I retired to bed for a deserved rest after a gentle towel-drying—an unexpected experience. Chasing anything will have to wait, as I recuperate.

We have returned to King's Bromley, and the end of our cruise although my diary remains unfinished. I shall update you on my recovery tomorrow.

Kings Bromley

 Just to round off yesterday, 13 September. I am not superstitious. My owners, clearly concerned for my state of health, took a gentle stroll with me around our beloved marina. It was a lovely evening and there are lots of really interesting walks here as some of you know. Rounding a bend, there was a big white cat sitting in the middle of my path right in front of me and in my way! Naturally, I barked at it, this is what I am meant to do. It took no notice, it did not flinch and so I barked again, still no response. I pranced around it in a sort of dance and tried again, ignoring my bearded one's cautionary remarks, whereupon the cat, much to my surprise, was able to respond in a very speedy and aggressive fashion. Forgetting any aches and pains, I took off!

I had the whiskered monster hanging on my tail. The next moment, the cat was safely up a tree, I could not climb trees. Instead, I found myself up to my neck in water, again. Ugh! I hate it when that happens. I managed to climb out through the reeds unaided! This demonstration of my agility confirmed that my earlier accident had caused me no damage. I was, however exceedingly embarrassed. Fancy getting wet like this twice in 24 hours, I suspect someone witnessed it. I did get another rub down, I like that and I slept for quite a while.

On our final evening at Kings Bromley: They are going out for dinner to The Boars Head, I know this is one of their favourite food houses. They have dinner with Mr Carvery and it is two for ten whatever that means! I can't work that out, sums are not for me. They are going to be joined by John, that would make three of them! He visited them yesterday when I had my accident. I am quite happy to guard the kennel or even my short-kennel as we have that back now. I chose my long-kennel as I will be leaving it soon, and I went to sleep. I heard them return quite late and I was happy.

My bearded one woke me up for his walk on our final morning at our marina, I did have a bit of a lie-in. I looked for the cat. He did not show his whiskery face again, I was quite relieved. I gave his long-kennel a wide berth.

The weather was dry this morning and so my bearded one was busy doing some painting of my long-kennel, touching up bits here and there doing some varnishing and mysterious things to the engine, under my bedroom. I know he got quite mucky, this often happens and my long-haired one tells him off, it seems he nearly always has the wrong clothes on. She has been busy doing great quantities of washing and stuff and packing things away. All this is I suppose preparing my long-kennel for the winter. I have been doing some more sleeping, keeping out of the way under the dining room table.

And so, my friends, it is with a heavy heart that I bid you farewell, at least for now. As I sit here with my loyal Pets, my companions, Jan, the one with the flowing mane, and Andrew, the proud bearer of a magnificent beard, we extend our deepest gratitude to all of you who ventured to meet us in person or who have managed to read about our grand escapades. We sincerely hope that our tales have brought you joy and amusement, for they certainly have to us!

Afterword

Once we had bidden farewell to my beloved long-kennel Albert in Staffordshire, with hopes of reuniting in the near future, we embarked on our, last for now, English adventure, venturing southward in Yeti, our trusty short-kennel. Our destination? Eastbourne, where we planned to revel in the company of family and friends for the final leg of our journey. And oh, what a journey it has been! My Pets tell me that before they lived in Spain, this was before I was born, they used to live in Eastbourne. So this will be fun! It is a place they love to visit.

As we traversed the picturesque landscapes, the weather graced us with an intriguing mixture and often a pleasant dry and sunny disposition. Allow me, to regale you with some of the highlights from our time in Eastbourne. Firstly, let me disclose I had many sleepovers in different places, my slumber was frequently interrupted, and my bed was shifted from one place to another. But fear not, for duty called! I diligently carried out my fox patrol duties, ever vigilant in protecting our encampment. And oh, the picnics and children's parties! A profusion of delectable morsels adorned the ground, though regrettably none were intended for my indulgence. Alas, such is life.

Amidst the festivities, I endured the curious proddings and pokes of countless little humans, their endless fascination with my presence unabated. Yet, I remained steadfast in my role, always ready to accompany my Pets and

their friends on invigorating hikes along the scenic paths particularly I enjoyed The South Downs, a curious description of the gentle but majestic hills in this part of Sussex. I must not forget to mention the splendid encounters with my fellow canines, a delightful abundance that left me with a wagging tail and a joyful heart.

Finally, the tale of the ill-fated ferry! It was on a Sunday, and we eagerly awaited our embarkation upon the colossal ferry kennel vessel that brought us here and was destined to return us to northern Spain. Alas, a most peculiar turn of events occurred—a strike action, if you can believe it! The details escape me, but the outcome was clear: our ferry did not sail. However, adversity only fuelled our determination, and alternative arrangements were swiftly made. We retraced our steps, driving in my short-kennel to a place near Ashford in Kent where my bearded one was directed and skilfully drove into a strange big box that turned out to be one of many making up a long rattling vehicle that they called a train. All together we descended beneath the English Channel.

Curiously, there were no windows and so I could see no fish and suddenly after only about half an hour, we arrived in a different country. Here we are back on the other side of the road again. I am going to have a snooze on the back seat. I am sure they know what they are doing. I leave this stuff to them. France and then Spain awaited our tireless exploration. We continued our journey in the comfort of my reliable short-kennel, with my Pets taking turns behind the wheel, which appeared to be necessary, and with frequent stops, I was afforded ample opportunities for short explorations and a few games along the way.

With two nights staying in different big bedroom houses it took us nearly three days to complete this continental escapade. While my Pets stayed alert and engaged, I found solace in my slumber, blissfully dreaming through most of our voyage. And now, as I reflect upon our grand odyssey, I can only say that it has been a journey filled with whimsy, camaraderie, and the delightful unpredictability that accompanies such endeavours. Until our paths cross again, dear reader, may your own journeys be filled with equal measures of excitement and tranquillity. Farewell for now!

END